Dresden Suite

by

Deloris H. Netzband

Savvy Press
Salem, NY

Published by Savvy Press http://www.savvypress.com

ISBN: 978-1-939113-21-4
LCCN: 2013944704

Printed in the United States of America

"Summering in Dresden" first appeared in Bloodroot Literary Magazine, vol. 1, 2008; "Slight Signs of Spring" first appeared in Bloodroot Literary Magazine, vol. 5, 2012; "Burning or Coming Down" first appeared in Confrontation, Summer1982; "A Resident of Dresden" first appeared in Confrontation, Issue 104, Summer 2009.

To the one with many names:

Aunt Lucy

Mama Lucy

Nana

My Mother

past me. I recognized her face when she sat down next to me. It was Mrs. Phillips, the department secretary. The coming attraction, a cop film replete with car chases and shoot-out with police officers and criminals hurling obscenities at each other, flickered images across the screen.

Though not a very good judge of women's ages, I estimated Mrs. Phillips to be in her fifties. She had the scrubbed, seriousness of a woman who always made note of phone calls, reminded people of meets at least twenty minutes before they began; in other words, totally efficient, unglamorous, and reliable. I, on the other hand, still have a boyishness that belies my age, or at least, I like to think so. She turned toward me and spoke naturally and calmly as though we were in the office.

"Good evening, Professor."

"Good evening, Mrs. Phillips."

The movie began. The music was so familiar because I had a cassette with the score that I played in my car whenever I went on long trips. After they left, I considered buying a Porsche (his car in the film), but the rigors of the New England winters decided me against a sports car. Instead, I drive a serviceable and reliable four-wheel drive vehicle. From the moment the film started, I was no longer myself, I became the character in it. I lost myself completely and hardly noticed Mrs. Phillips or her reaction to it.

When the film was over and the lights came up, I noticed that she was still seated next to me though the theater was nearly empty. Her face was flushed and her eyes puffy from crying. It touched me to see that she had been so swept away by the film and reminded me of my wife's reaction to it.

"Mrs. Phillips," I asked, "Would you be interested in having a cup of coffee with me?"

"Why thank you, Professor," she answered in her even secretarial voice.

I helped her into her coat and took her arm as we left the theater. We decided to leave our cars in the parking lot and walk to a nearby cafe. The town was already closed down though it wasn't even ten o'clock. The night was cold and snow hung expectantly in the air. The cafe was even more barren than the movie theater had been. Mrs. Phillips stood for a long time staring at the pastry that looked slightly wilted and bruised behind the glass counter.

"Go ahead," I encouraged. I imagined that she worried about her weight, though she couldn't be considered overweight. She was not, however, the slender model type that I must confess I usually find so attractive. My wife once accused me of falling in love with her when she had pneumonia and regretting the fact that she had ever recovered and regained her robust healthy look. Not that she was ever anything but waifishly thin. I must admit she was much prettier thin than fat, but I thought that Mrs. Phillips looked best with some weight on her. The women who populated my life since I have been alone have all been tall and thin. A colleague of mine from my early days in Dresden was accused of trying to score with the entire secretarial staff at Amberton. He did not serve as a model for me. Instead, I reserved my conquests to nurses at the Rebecca Amberton Memorial Hospital. My longest relationship was with Wendy Vogel, the real estate agent who sold my house and got me my condo. I made a pact with myself that I wouldn't pursue students, any of the secretarial staff, or even a colleague (though I was less adamant on the last score.) Where did that leave Mrs. Phillips? She was at least a decade my senior. I reasoned that this was only coffee, not romance.

We sat at a table by the frosted window and looked out on the deserted street of the town where there was no one to see or judge us.

After the coffee, I said, "I think I'll have a beer."

She decided on the walnut cake that she ate slowly; taking sips of tea with it.

"Go ahead," she said to me. "Beer makes me feel cold."

"Does it?" I questioned as I got up to go for the beer.

When I returned, I asked, "How did you like the film?"

"It was very good," she said hesitantly. "I don't go to the

movies often. Was it an old one?"

"Yes. The first time I saw it was when I lived in New York."

"You lived in New York too?" she inquired. "I lived there years ago when I got married."

"Really," I said with interest. I wanted to know more about her, to find out why she had been so shaken by the film. She had admitted that she didn't go to films much and she didn't have the same kind of attachment to them that I did. I had the belief that levelheaded secretaries didn't as a rule cry in movies without a logical explanation.

"Do you miss New York?" I asked. A strange expression crossed her face, a kind of melancholy that was mixed with nostalgia for some secret remembrance.

"New York . . . Oh, that's ancient history . . . a lifetime ago . . . I was just a girl. I married and we went to New York."

"Where are you from?" I was eager to get to the bottom of her mystery. She looked younger than I had estimated. There was something almost girlish in her mannerism and expression that I found both charming and pitiable. She avoided my gaze and looked down at her hands. She fidgeted nervously with the mug filled with what must by now have been lukewarm tea.

"I was born in Brattleboro," she said after a while. "He was an actor doing summer stock near there," she continued almost as though to herself. "At the end of the summer, we went to New York . . . I was just a girl, just a few years out of high school."

"And you stayed there until you came up here," I put in.

"No, I was only in New York for a very short time," she told me in a halting voice.

The same stricken look I had seen on her face after the movie returned. I then did something uncharacteristic of me. I reached out and took her hand. It was cold and damp. I tried to think of something reassuring to say to her. It hit me that we weren't even on a first name basis and yet I knew she was going to tell me something painful and intimate.

"He died," she said quietly. "It was sudden. The doctors weren't sure what caused it. He just died."

Abruptly, she stopped talking, and tried to get her hand away from mine. I wouldn't release it.

"That's why the movie," I began.

"We never made love," she interrupted. For the first time, she looked at me, eagerly searching my face for some reaction. I held her hand more tightly.

"My first name is . . ." I started nervously without acknowledging what she had revealed to me.

"I know your name, Professor," she interrupted and added, "His name was Stefan."

"No," I gasped taken aback.

"We were married for a month and we never made love," she repeated in a hushed tone. There was hurt, disappointment, and anguish on her face. I feared she would begin to cry again, but she didn't. Suddenly, I wasn't sure if her first name was Margaret or Marjorie. All the older professors called her Marg.

"Margaret," I said finally assured that was her name. "I'm sorry. You know that film had a lot of memories for me too. Some of them were painful too."

"Why did you see it again?" she asked.

Her question took me by surprise. "I like it," I said awkwardly, "I like films very much."

"But seeing a film over and over again is like reliving an unhappy experience," she said.

"Not for me," I said. I didn't think going into my need for an active fantasy life would be appropriate at the time.

"There's enough ugliness, enough pain in the world without going to the movies to see it," she remarked.

"Before I could respond fully, the owner came around to tell us that it was closing time. We walked back to the parking lot without speaking. Parting, we exchanged farewells.

"See you tomorrow," I called uncertain if she heard me since she was already in her car. The cold brittle night forced me into my car and away from her.

I had a hard time getting to sleep. I thought of Marsha Fishbein, the first girl I ever had sex with. It had started in the balcony of the Loew's Rialto on the Grand Concourse and progressed to her bedroom in her parents' apartment several blocks away. For some reason, I remember I was wearing the previous day's boxer shorts. It was unmemorable sex, quick and not at all personable.

I kissed her and she said, "Your lips are so soft and big, like a Negro's. Not that I ever kissed a Negro . . . We're like Romeo and Juliet," she announced.

It took me a long time to make the connection. At first, I thought she believed that I was a Negro. Then I realized that she was Jewish and she figured I was Catholic because I was Italian. I was nothing. My family, even my mother, was not anti-religious, just not religious. Marsha and I never became an item, nor did we repeat that first experience. I think I executed the act with some sophistication. There was no one I could tell. I was sixteen and that was pretty late for boys in my neighborhood of the Bronx or so the mythology went. I have had only one great passion of my life. I tossed and turned in bed and shifted my thoughts to Margaret Phillips and what she had told me about herself. The last word that I remembered before I finally went to sleep was never.

Although I didn't have classes until the afternoon and office hours after that, I forced myself to get out of bed early and headed to the English Department without breakfast. Margaret was at her desk, fresh and crisp as usual. Her greeting was warm and friendly, but still more or less formal.

"Good morning, Professor."

I searched her face for some secret sarcasm but dismissed the thought from my mind. She was just a careful and cautious individual who wouldn't take unfair advantage.

"Good morning, Margaret. Is there any coffee yet?"

"I believe Professor Dworkins is making some. It should be ready by now," she replied without looking at me.

I wondered if she was embarrassed though she didn't behave at all in that manner. Then it came to me that I was the one who was acting peculiar.

"Margaret, would you have dinner with me?" I blurted out.

"Certainly, if you'd like," she answered softly. She looked up at me and said in a soothing voice, "Professor . . . if you have appointments, you should be getting to your office."

"Thank you, Margaret," I replied, "thank you."

The rest of the day was passed in a fog. I rarely do anything without planning it and so I was riddled with doubts and misgivings about my sudden impulse to proceed with Margaret beyond the lines I had drawn.

We had dinner at The Fields Inn twelve miles outside of Dresden. As we drove back, we didn't talk much. There seemed to be nothing to say. I had been aware all evening that she had taken great pains with her hair, her face, and her clothes. In the office, she wore next to no makeup and never was there even the vaguest hint of anything more scented than hand lotion about her. The perfume, the makeup added a mystery to her that was exciting. Eagerly, I accepted her invitation to come in for a drink when we reached her house.

"This is a very cozy place you have here."

"Thank you. Many of the older pieces of furniture are from my parents' home. When my mother passed away, all of us had our pick of the things we wanted."

She glanced wistfully around the room and seemed to evaluate the items once again. I was touched with a mixture of admiration and pity for her gestures and expression as she moved around her small comfortable house.

"I like old houses and old things," I confessed. "You'd never know it. I live in an ultra modern apartment."

"You live out in the condos on Lake Drive, don't you?"

"Yes. I once lived in a house on the other side of the lake."

"About last night," she began.

"You don't owe me an explanation," I interrupted.

"I've never talked about my husband before," she continued.

"I understand."

"You see, I was a very young girl. Life had been so safe, so ordinary for me before Stefan. My family had lived in the same town for generations. Stefan came from a different world, out of what seemed to be a different time. And then it was over before it had ever become quite real. He was dead and it was over. There wasn't even anything to remember. I went home, went to Business College and expected to fall back into my life, but I couldn't. Just that brief moment with Stefan changed me forever. Do you know what I mean?"

"I think so," I said reluctantly. She had that look again. She was both old and young.

"Years go by like the changing seasons," she said sadly. She didn't look as though she would cry. I was glad of that because I knew I was incapable of stopping her tears.

"You know why I like films," I said changing the subject, "they make me understand more about the world and about myself at a distance. I have a lot to understand."

"Most of the other professors your age like skiing and running."

"I suppose so . . . I play tennis," I added hurriedly.

"I thought a lot about the movie," she said. "I think I liked it too. I probably wouldn't have cried if I didn't like it. It's strange to meet someone who cares about made-up people in a make-believe world more than real ones."

"I care about real people. I have a son," I explained. I knew I should stop talking, but I couldn't. "Still filmgoers identify with the made-up people and that's what makes us cry because we see our own suffering and pain in theirs." I thought I sounded like a college professor giving a lecture but I didn't feel that way.

"I suppose you're right. It's true I was reminded of Stefan in the movie. He was so glamorous and mysterious. Everything was a great adventure for him. I was always happy with him. I thought I'd never be sad. And then it was over. It doesn't seem fair."

I reached out and took her in my arms. My leg got caught under the coffee table and sent a glass tumbling to the floor. It didn't break, but I released her.

"I'm sorry," I mumbled. It wasn't going well, at least not the way it would go if I were anywhere close to my film image of myself.

"It's all right," she said. There was an eager look in her eyes. She brushed the hair off her forehead. I thought I saw a touch of enchantment in her eyes.

"It's all right," she said again. This time she got up from the couch and reached out her hands to me. Without saying anything else, I knew what she meant. It was all right that I wasn't a handsome actor, racecar driver, or tennis player. I was just an Amberton professor who wrote boring pedantic papers. And it was all right that she wasn't a young beautiful widow or my beloved. It wasn't Brazil, only Dresden, a college town in New England. Still we surrendered to the sound of imaginary Brazilian music pulsating all around us.

Summering in Dresden

At first, Dresden was known for Amberton College, a small elite women's college, cradled between the White and Green Mountains. Then in some circles Dresden became known for the Rebecca Amberton Mental Health Clinic, which was a well-known retreat for rehabilitating celebrities. A less well-known attribute of Dresden is its reputation as a safe and comfortable haven for families, especially for the well-educated and affluent. The college, the medical center, and more recently the influx of high tech industries, have brought an increase in young families. The public schools expanded and the need for a recreational program led to the building and establishment of the Dresden Recreational Complex. Back in 1957, a group of investors converted a natural pond at the northern end of Dresden into a man-made lake, ideal for ice skating in winter and swimming in summer. Later, a sports complex and tennis courts were added.

Summering in Dresden became ideal. Long days, lush green trees, picnic tables, tents pitched in the woods, and the rolling hills of the Dresden Country Club golf course had a magic aura about them. But most of all the happy cheerful voices of the children of Dresden made summer idyllic.

The place that most exemplifies a Dresden summer is the lake. One side of it has the recreational area, the beach, the tennis courts, and the sports complex. On the other side are the condos and summer cottages.

The hub of activity on a summer day is on the beach at the water's edge where the Dresden children go to play. They are guarded mostly by the mothers who sit watchfully alert. Some of them wear bikinis, but mostly their sleek oiled bodies are in one-piece suits. There is the smell of suntan lotion, perspiration, lemonade, and privilege about them. Bottles, Popsicle sticks, paper cups, newspapers, and the latest New York Times bestsellers are strewn along the beach. Towels are their flags—they proclaim Cracker Jack, Snoopy, Uncola, Scooby Doo. These maternal sentinels watch over the tight little bodies in red, green, purple, yellow, and blue bathing suits, with the straps tied together by a shoestring, with their red peeling shoulders, damp blond, red, and brown hair plastered against boy and girl heads.

It's summering in Dresden.

There is a watchful waiting that seems relaxed, but really isn't. Some of the women play cards. The one or two men read newspapers. Buckets, pails, shovels, and sand chairs clutter the water's edge. Tiny fingers push into the sand all the way past the hot dry cutting grains into the wet damp moisture underneath. Giggles, cries, and whines issue forth from a polyglot of faces. The wiggling, squirming mass of childhood is playing on the beach.

Watching over them are not just the lifeguards perched high on the chairs with whistles hanging around their confident athletic suntanned necks, but the real guards—the mothers.

It's mothering in Dresden.

Each year there is at least one near drowning. One mishap that for Dresden takes on the magnitude of the crop of murders one expects in urban areas. This is no shark attack fantasy like the popular movie and its sequels. This is real tragedy in this modern-day Eden. Some little girlbody, boybody sinks beneath the dark lake waters and is almost lost in the secure gated world of privilege. It is hard to change the rituals of summering, even if the ultimate loss occurs. The vigilance may increase for a time. Perhaps you might see alarm flicker across otherwise tranquil faces until the summer ends. But everyone feels so safe, so entitled to the privileges of paradise.

It's sorrowing in Dresden.

Claire Lowell's station wagon pulled onto the grassy knoll facing the sports complex. She was late. It was Timmy's last lesson. He had to swim from the shore to the raft in the middle of the lake and back. She wanted to be there to spur him on. Timmy had come out earlier with his best friend, Scott Macklin.

In many ways, Claire is different from the typical Dresden mother. There is much of the free spirit about her. For instance, she wears her bathing suit while driving her car. A beach towel separates her body from the leather seat. She pushed her short black hair out of her eyes and reached for a cigarette in the straw bag next to her. The pack was empty. Just, as well, she told herself, she was trying to quit. As she got out of the car, her feet were half in and half out of her sandals. She hated shoes and only wore them because her husband Tim continually lectured her about driving barefoot.

She looked for Timmy. The sun was directly overhead. She held her hand over her eyebrow trying to shade her eyes. Claire hated sunglasses. She thought they all looked cheap and tacky on her. After a certain age no one could wear sunglasses and look anything but ridiculous, she thought. She wasn't sophisticated or stylish, but she had her standards.

Claire looked for Timmy among the dozen or so children on the shore. It was hard to distinguish him from any of the other little squirmy, wiggly boys and girls of nine and ten. She had promised her son she would come to watch him swim. She knew he would have preferred his father to be there, but that was impossible. Tim had important things to do.

Slowly she walked across the asphalt parking area, dodging in between cars. The sounds of the summer wafted in and out of her consciousness. She hoped that Timmy hadn't taken his test yet. He needed to be encouraged. This was the one thing in the sports arena he had even ventured to try. He had to succeed and if he did, Claire thought then perhaps she could convince Tim to come to the lake and watch Timmy swim on the weekend. She paused at the entrance of the fenced-in area of the beach, took her sandals completely off, and dropped them into her straw beach bag.

As she moved closer to the crowd of children on the beach, she was able to distinguish one from another. Scott Macklin, Debby Washburn, Ben Taylor, Xanda Wyatt, and Wally Mitford. Standing there together, they looked the same, though the names were distinct and they all went to their separate houses, to their separate mothers and fathers at the end of the day. Timmy was not among them. Claire was annoyed. She had missed Timmy's turn, she feared. She looked out to the raft. Even at a distance, she did distinguish her son Timmy from the other boys. His slight slender body and rounded shoulders stood out somehow from the others. She sighed with both relief and disappointment, at least she could watch him swim back.

To her left sat a cluster of women with infants. It was impossible to determine the sex of any of the babies or who the individual mothers were.

Babylove in Dresden

Claire looked once more toward the raft. She had misplaced Timmy again. He wasn't on the raft. She supposed he was in the water. She spotted him. Swimming alongside him was an older boy. Claire assumed the older boy was the lifeguard. Timmy seemed to be having trouble. She had hoped against hope that he would be able to sail through the test. Obviously, he hadn't. Her heart sank. The lifeguard's strokes were smooth and easy while Timmy's were choppy and uneven. Timmy's thin, slight arms reached nervously out of the water. It was a struggle for him. Slowly, he made his way to the shore. Panic went through her, along with disappointment. She had wanted so much for her son to succeed. He could have drowned. She admonished herself. At least, he's safe, she thought. That was the most important thing. Not that his father would agree. His father would be annoyed by Timmy's awkwardness. She watched as Timmy stumbled from the water onto the beach. The next child who stood waist deep in the water was given the signal by the lifeguard to proceed to the raft. Claire made her way rapidly to her son's side.

"Mom, you came after all," he called to her.

"I promised, didn't I?"

"Gee, I wasn't very good . . . I sucked," he said.

"Timmy, don't say 'sucked'," she said before she hugged him and handed him a towel from her beach bag. She put her arm around his wet shoulders. He was cold, and it made her shiver.

"I made you cold, Mom," he said looking up at her.

"No. I guess I should go into the water myself. I haven't been swimming all summer. Is it very cold?"

"It's all right," he said. There was something sad and almost adult in his voice.

"Are you going to stick around much longer?" he asked her.

"No, honey. I'll just take a quick swim and get back to the house. You can come back with the Macklins later. Is that all right?"

"Sure, Mom . . . See ya."

He turned from her and headed down the beach. Suddenly he turned back toward her and said, "Can I have another dollar?" he asked.

"Timmy, we had an agreement. You have to live with your allowance and any money that you earn doing chores," she scolded.

"I know, Mom, but I wanted to go in with Scott and some of the other guys for a pizza."

"Yuck," she replied, "The pizzas they make here are terrible."

"Don't say 'yuck'," he smiled.

Claire reached into her straw bag and took out a small purse. She handed her son a dollar.

He ran off toward the clubhouse.

It's summering at the lake.

Claire tried to think of how she would explain Timmy's poor performance to his father. She needed to clear her head. A swim would do that. She headed for the water, but it was packed with small children doing their swimming tests. It would be another half hour or more before she could go in without them. Claire decided she would hike up to the northern end of the lake. Generally, it was a place where people went fishing or took a canoe out on the water and was regarded as still in its primitive state. Claire liked to swim there. She had been swimming there since she was a young girl. It was her special place. When she reached its somewhat rocky shore, she put down her straw bag and walked into the water. The water felt cold and good against her hot sticky skin. She could stop worrying about Timmy momentarily. The noise and clatter was far from her at the other end of the lake. She let her body give way to the water, swimming easily, steadily, and with assurance. Claire reached an old raft without effort. She stood on it and looked south toward the crowded end of the lake. She could have swum to the crowded end of the lake easily. Claire had been a champion swimmer when she was a teenager. She wished some of that had rubbed off on Timmy. Maybe she could bring him here and give him some private lessons, she thought as she dove into the water.

It seemed colder than before and her strokes became more labored. She swam into a cold stream that caused a cramp in her leg. Claire didn't struggle for long or cry out. She went down slowly, sinking silently to the bottom, never to come up again.

It's summering in Dresden

At five, cars started pulling out of the parking lot. By five-thirty, over half the cars were gone. By a quarter to seven, Claire Lowell's station wagon was alone in its spot facing the empty sports complex. By seven-thirty, twilight fell across her straw bag on the deserted sandy beach at the northern-most tip of the lake. At eight, the Dresden police car drove through the gate. Tim Lowell sat silently next to the policeman.

Timmy was at Scott Macklin's eating hamburgers cooked on the outdoor grill by Scott's father Jack. Timmy tried not to think about how poorly he had done at the lake. He knew it was all right with his mother, but his father was a different story. His father would give him that disappointed look that meant he had failed him again.

Timmy looked up to see his father standing next to Mr. and Mrs. Macklin at the grill. Mr. Macklin put his hand on his father's shoulder. Mrs. Macklin raised her hands to hide her face. Timmy heard a strange sound come from Mrs. Macklin, something between a moan and the word "no." Then he saw them look his way and saw them come toward him. He wanted to run, but he couldn't move.

It's paradise lost in Dresden

Slight Signs of Spring

Snow still covered much of the mountaintops, but in the clearings there were some spring flowers bravely starting to bud. Spring is a long time coming up North and short when it does arrive. Still, for me, it is the sweetest of all seasons because it can awaken even the dullest and most deadened. Perhaps that's why I listened to my friend Vicki. Otherwise I would never have found myself in this situation.

I've been divorced for over a decade, so I'm out of it and have been for years. I live alone in a small house about twenty miles north of Dresden with a couple of very independent animals to keep me company. I've lost the knack of relationships. But my friend Vicki has assured me that it's like riding a bicycle and that I'll get the hang of it all over again as soon as I get back on the bike. I'm not so certain. I'm not even certain I want to.

But Vicki's persistence made me acquiesce. Going on a blind date at my age is a major mistake, no matter what Vicki says. All I can think about are the dreadful blind dates I had in college. After Simon and I started dating, I told myself I would never again go on a blind date. I didn't have to. I married Simon. Now Simon is history, and I am older but not much wiser, getting ready for a blind date arranged by my friend Vicki.

"You have a lot in common," Vicki told me over lunch at the Dresden Inn.

"What?" I inquired.

"You're both fugitives from the city. You left the pressures and exhilaration of the city to pursue the artistic life in the North Country. Jared Hale is a novelist, and you are a potter and sculptor."

"Jared Hale." I said. "That name sounds familiar."

"He won the Hathorn or one of those other prizes in the late seventies, early eighties," Vicki told me.

"You mean he's a successful artist and I'm up here struggling to make ends meet, working as a substitute teacher to pay bills."

"Don't sell yourself short," Vicki encouraged.

"I'm a realist, Vicki."

Vicki put her hands up to her ears and said, "I can't hear you."

I knew it was hopeless to argue with her. She was dead set on matchmaking, and I was one of her projects.

"Jared's renting a house with the idea of buying it. He came into the shop and spotted some of your bowls and nearly flipped. So I said, 'If you like her bowls, you're going to love her.'"

"What did he say? I bet he thought you were crazy."

"No, he didn't. He checked out the bottom of one of the bowls and looked at your signature. 'Maura.' he said. 'Is that her first name or last?' I told him that you were somewhat of a mystery. You only admit to having one name."

I laughed. It was nothing mysterious. I couldn't bring myself to use my married name now that I was divorced; but my maiden name was some twenty years in the past in what seemed like another lifetime.

"So tell me something about him," I said as we sipped coffee. Vicki reached into her large purse and took out a paperback book.

"Read this," she said. "This is his first novel. It's about some Harvard dropouts living in Newton or Somerville. It's full of angst about Vietnam, Watergate, and all that. First thing I want you to do is look at his picture."

Vicki shoved the paperback at me. I looked at his picture. "Doesn't he look like the French actor Jean-Louis Trintignant?" she asked.

"Vicki, this picture must be over fifteen years old. I hope you haven't shown him any old pictures of me. There's such a thing as truth in advertising."

"No, darling. You forget, I haven't known you fifteen years. And let me just say that he has matured divinely. He has all the right lines in his chiseled face. Those sad brown eyes. Gray at the temples."

"You chose the one actor I can't resist," I replied. "Still, you keep saying we have so much in common."

"You do," Vicki insisted. "He's divorced too. His ex-wife is Marisa Hale, the opera singer. She's made the big step from Boston to New York in the opera world. I remember reading about them when Fred and I lived in Boston. They were a sparkling couple — she, a rising young mezzo-soprano, and he the gifted young writer. Now she's in New York and he's up here. After a long time, his second novel was published, and now he's working on his third book. I ordered the new novel, and the bookstore says it'll be in by the end of the week."

Vicki leaned forward toward me and said, "I think he was terribly battered. Divorce. Writer's block."

"Who hasn't been battered?" I shot back at her. "All of us aren't as lucky as you in the marriage game."

"Oh, Fred and I, we're just too old to change partners. But let me tell you, if I was free, I'd set my sights for Jared. He's smoldering," Vicki said.

"I don't know if I'm up for that," I replied.

"Oh sure you are." "Besides, you can tell he has suffered. He was a golden boy for a time, and then the times changed and he was no longer in vogue."

I was tempted to tell Vicki that Jared was more the fool for not sensing the change of taste and changing with it. I held my peace, however, because Vicki doesn't take criticism well. Instead, she thrives on understanding other people's tragedies and substituting them for her own emotional life. Vicki allows herself to take dangerous plunges into other people's emotional maelstroms.

Recently, I think I've noticed something creeping into Vicki and Fred's relationship. It's hard to explain, but it seems like there is a sense of unease between them. It could be my imagination. I try to push the thought away because I need for them to be all right. Then I can forget my own failures and broken promises. For years, I was the pretty, artistic, rather spacey wife of an investment banker — not taken seriously, not taking myself seriously. I loved my husband. I even loved him after the divorce. I just couldn't live with him. I didn't feel authentic, real, or alive. I went in search of myself, and when I attempted to return he wouldn't take me back. On my own, I was first drawn to Dresden and the Amberton College community and then to my little house and the animals. It was easy to let time pass and not face the arena of marriage and relationships.

In the days before my date, I often glanced at Jared's picture and marveled at his dark good looks. It helped to spark excitement in me to meet the grown-up, older version of him.

As I prepared to go out, I realized that I'd lost the knack of makeup at an age when I could use it. I brushed my hair with its gray and silver strands, not many, but too numerous to be plucked away and forgotten. It was hard to decide what to wear. I decided I needed something that would shield my true self from the close scrutiny of a stranger. I had nothing in my wardrobe that could do that. After so many years in the North Country, my closet was filled with jeans, flannel shirts, and boots. By contrast, my years in the city were filled with stylish clothes or whimsical pieces from antique clothing stores, expensive shoes, and my hair long and flowing down my back. I left all that behind me, telling myself it was a disguise of my true self. I wondered, as I settled for a plaid skirt and a dark mock turtleneck with sensible walking shoes, if these were disguises too. I looked like I was going to either substitute teach or on a job interview. I changed clothes again, leaving on the dark top, and putting on dark faux-suede pants and ankle boots — the closest thing to fashion I owned. Even these clothes were at least seven years old.

On top of everything, my conversation skills were rusty. I did make a mental note to avoid the familiar country chatter. I didn't intend to dwell on wood stoves or talk about planting my garden in a few weeks. These were the worn coinage of country life. Those of us without children, and some with them, continually recited the triumphs and failures that we have had with nature. Which wood-burning stove was superior? Which four-wheel drive vehicle was essential for survival in the winter and mud season? What were the tried and true methods of dealing with cabin fever?

Another big topic, of course, was the weather. It was usually centered around the winter. Few were concerned with the most popular season for the tourists — the fall. Some people deny that there is a spring, but I believe in it. Not just mud season with all its miseries, but the season of awakening. I believe in it and have seen slight signs of spring.

On the other hand, we were all flatlanders who took pride in the fact we'd chosen this life over the city. Yet we lamented our losses — good theater, current films, and the sense of being at the hub of style and fashion. For some the feeling of safety, the wholesomeness of life, or the idea of developing one's character and inner resources in a challenging environment compensated for the losses.

Fred and Vicki lived in a farmhouse that was over one hundred fifty years old. There were two ways to get to their house from mine. The faster way was gravel and dirt road almost all the way. The other way's longer, but I needed to travel on the dirt road uphill for only two miles. I chose the longer way, but I reminded myself not to discuss this. Jared must have heard enough about routes and ways in the four months he had lived here. Fred, I knew, must have discussed his commute of sixteen miles to his dental practice in Dresden. Just as Vicki had discussed how she decorated and restored old houses for new urban transplants. These were the things we talked about whenever I had dinner with them.

What else was there? I didn't know the state of art criticism, nor did I have anything original to say about violence in films. I had no new knowledge to bring to these topics. What could be discussed with some clarity, of course, was relationships. Vicki liked to think of herself as an authority, and Fred felt he was liberated enough as a man to talk about them too. But was that too presumptuous since

Jared and I were meeting for the first time. It was a strange thing to say, but in some ways relationships was the safest topic after all.

"How did you come?" Vicki asked as I entered the door.

"The long way," I answered.

"There was no need. The roads are fine," she scolded.

"Darling, you know that Maura is a Nervous Nelly," Fred chimed in.

I shoved a bottle of wine at him in hopes that he would get my not-so-subtle body language on the topic of my driving.

Jared stepped out from behind him. He was taller and more slightly built than I'd expected. The face, I saw, was older and more worn than the picture on the book jacket, but he was still a striking man. His world-weary expression looked better on him than it would on a woman.

"I'm Jared," he said extending his hand.

"I'm Maura."

"You two get acquainted while Fred and I put the finishing touches on dinner."

I sat on the couch. Jared took Fred's cozy burnt-orange leather chair that faced the fireplace.

"How long have you been up here?" Jared asked. "I'm just assuming you're not a native."

He had the husky voice of a former cigarette smoker.

"Ten years," I said. "I thought of moving to California and chose New England instead."

"Why?" he asked.

"I don't think I'm a California person."

"Neither am I. I went out there when they optioned my novel for a screenplay. All that sun annoyed me."

He paused for a moment and added, "Forget I said that. That's not my line. Someone gave it to me and I thought I'd use it, but it really doesn't sound like me."

"I like it," I said. "Did you get it especially for this evening, or was it just one of those things in your repertoire to be pulled out at the appropriate occasion?"

"It was years ago, and I haven't recited memorized lines to a girl since I was in high school," he apologized.

"Do you mind if I use it?" I asked.

"Well, no," he smiled.

"Not only am I not a California person, the sun annoys me," I tried out the expression myself.

He laughed. I felt comfortable with him. I hoped he felt comfortable with me.

Fred entered the room. "Nothing wrong with the wine you brought, Maura, but I think a chilled chardonnay goes better with the asparagus chicken," he told me.

We sat at the large oak dining table and savored the meal. Fred and Vicki kept the conversation going between them. I was aware that she was more flustered than usual.

"Vicki and her clients," Fred explained, "all that money and no taste."

"I should think that would suit you just fine," I replied. "Especially since they don't care how you spend it."

"Maura, you don't understand," Fred said as he patted Vicki's hand, "Does she, darling? Vicki suffers because she has to work among the Philistines."

Vicki didn't answer him but lightly kissed his cheek. All of us were silent for a moment. Vicki spoke first, "Fred, I think you need to get some more wood for the fire. Take Jared with you."

"Yes, dear," he answered.

As soon as they left, Vicki cornered me, "Well, what do you think of him?"

"He's nice," I replied.

"Maura, how unimaginative!" she snapped. "Why, he's marvelous! You know that behind his quiet brooding facade is a really profound mind."

"How do you know that?"

"I just know. Look at the way he listens, really listens to you.

Most men don't listen to women that way."

She grasped my hand. Her hands were moist with perspiration, her eyes alive with excitement.

"Don't you think he's attractive?" she urged. It wasn't really a question.

"Yes." Something about her demeanor prevented me from answering more fully.

"I'm disappointed in you, Maura. You aren't trying. Don't let the moment slip through your fingers."

"What are you talking about, Vicki?"

"You can't be happy stuck out here in the country alone. I know I wouldn't be! It's tragic! You need someone. Seize the moment."

There is something almost desperate in her voice.

"What do you want from me?" I questioned.

"Maura dear, I'm just concerned, that's all."

"How strange. This is the first time in the years we have known each other that you have been interested in my social life," I laughingly chastised her.

"That's not true. Besides, Jared's the most promising man to show up around here in years." She paused for a moment. "If I hadn't been married to Fred forever and didn't love him like one loves a pair of old shoes, I'd go for Jared myself."

"I know — you told me that before," I said in a puzzled voice.

"Jared is my kind of man," Vicki revealed.

"I find that hard to believe since he's so very different from Fred."

"You say that because you don't really know Fred. He has much of the dreamer and artist in him. His family forced him into dentistry. It was Fred's idea to move here before the city devoured and destroyed us and our marriage. But he's still caught up in his practice, and his only outlet is studying wines and his gardening."

Fred and Jared entered the room, interrupting our conversation.

"Do you realize that there are asparagus beds that were planted in the time of Henry, the Eighth that are still producing today? So you see, Jared, those sketches of my asparagus trenches are my investment in immortality."

"Perhaps I should invest in something like asparagus too. Something that will never go out of print," Jared smiled wistfully.

"Jared, be serious," Vicki said. "True art like yours lasts forever."

Vicki squeezed Jared's hand. There was an awkward pause. I couldn't think of anything to say though I wanted to say something to Jared to draw his attention away from Vicki and toward me. Vicki was the first one to break the silence.

"I know how important one's work is to an artist," Vicki exclaimed.

"Of course, you do, dear," Fred agreed in an obviously sarcastic tone.

"Don't make fun, Fred. In my small way I'm an artist too. Jared and Maura aren't the only ones. You make fun, yet you try to be an artist yourself, Why else do you waste your time on this pretentious nonsense about Renaissance gardening? What do you know about the Renaissance; you're from Brooklyn."

There was an ugly smile on her face. Clearly, the seeds of an old quarrel were rising to the surface. I knew I didn't want to be present for this. I looked at Jared. Neither did he.

He said, " I think I should be going, but I am without a car."

"I can drive you," I told him.

Vicki looked at me as though I have struck her in the face. "I brought Jared over here," she told me.

I wanted to reply that I was just seizing the moment.

"You should take the back road near the Dam," she instructed.

Jared embraced her politely, and she held on to him for just a moment longer than seemed necessary. Fred stood stone faced beside her.

"You sure you'll be all right on that road?" he asked.

"I have four-wheel drive too, Fred," I reminded him.

"Good night, Vicki." I turned and shook Fred's hand, "Good night, Fred, and thanks to both of you for a very nice evening."

Jared took my arm as we left the porch and went to my car. He stopped and looked up at the luminous moon and a sky full of stars.

"I had forgotten there were such stars," he said.

As we wound our way slowly along the muddy road away from Fred and Vicki, he asked me, "Have you known them long?"

"Since they came here about eight years ago."

"Such sad people," he said.

"Why do you say that?"

"They're trying so hard to convince themselves that they're happy and failing so miserably."

"How damned presumptuous of you!"

"Of course, you're perfectly right. It's just that I've been there myself. I know that place so well."

"You have no right," I told him with less heat. I could see he wasn't being cruel. There was such sadness in his voice and eyes. I softened a little.

"Divorced people should never look at marriage," I told him.

"Other people's marriages are always easier to see than one's own," he said.

"I try not to look too deeply at anything anymore," I confessed.

"I think you do, but you have more taste than to discuss your friends with a virtual stranger. Forgive my rudeness."

"Forgiven."

"I think they'll be very disappointed if we don't see each other again," Jared said.

I wondered if that was true. Earlier I believed Vicki wanted to be a matchmaker. Now I wondered.

"We'll see each other again, I'm sure," I said after a moment.

"I guess I didn't get my point across very well. I was using Vicki and Fred as an excuse to shield myself against your possible rejection of another date. It goes along with my lame attempts to be witty before. Now I'm asking you straight out — maybe when the weather is better — would you like to see me again?"

"Very much, Jared. But let's not talk about Fred and Vicki ever again."

"Agreed," he replied.

We both knew that we more than likely would break that pact. It was hard not to talk about relationships, especially when you were trying to develop your own. We said good night at the side of the road. His driveway was too muddy for me to take him to his doorway. Maybe next time.

Summer Help

The summer of my junior year at Amberton College, I worked as a waitress at the Fields. The Fields Inn was twelve miles south of Dresden in a tiny village that was a strange combination of resort and mill town, which is what it had been at the turn of the century. I went there largely because my college roommate Susan Hughes had offered me her condo in Dresden for the summer. Also she told me that the Fields was an excellent place to earn money as a waitress in both the summer and winter. Susie was in Switzerland working at an exclusive summer camp that she had attended as a child. The Fields wasn't quite the gold mine Susie had predicted. The mainstay of the Inn was busloads of senior citizens traveling on package tours through New England. But there were other compensations. I was an art major at Amberton, and I would be able to paint and live in a luxurious place while I did it. Besides, I would get to know something about how real people lived.

All the other summer help, as well as the permanent staff, were local residents who had lived there all their lives and would probably die there. Dorothy, who was training me, was typical of the permanent employees. She was a taciturn woman who rarely smiled. Our conversation consisted mostly of her telling me what I was doing wrong. Like her coworkers, she was unaccustomed to strangers and instantly mistrusted them. Not only was I a stranger because I grew up on Long Island in New York, I was a stranger because I was an Amberton student from the college town of Dresden. The mistrust and dislike of the town of Dresden and its Amberton College belied the fact that it was only a few miles away.

When I first started to work at the Fields, I would hop in my car and go home during the long break between lunch and dinner. I decided after a while that it would be good to stay and spend time with my coworkers. Dorothy's best friend was Thelma, an energetic blonde with a heavy bosom. I had thought both of them in their mid to late thirties and was surprised to discover that Thelma was only in her late twenties.

"Pete committed suicide," I overheard Thelma tell Dorothy one quiet afternoon when we were setting up dinner for three busloads of "golden-agers" from New Jersey.

"Weren't no accident. Pete called me the day before he did it," Thelma seemed to boast. "He really loved me . . . Only married Leanne cause she was pregnant. Used to call me all the time, even after they were married."

Dorothy looked skeptical. "Thelma Yvonne Whittier, Pete run off with Leanne long before she had that baby. He left you high and dry and you and everybody else knows it!"

Thelma shrugged her shoulders. "A person can make a mistake. He loved me," she insisted.

"He had a funny way of showing it," Dorothy replied.

"I know what I know. I wouldn't have married Pete anyway. He drank too much."

"I feel sorry for Leanne with those children and him dead," Dorothy said.

"Leanne will be all right. You know she was stepping out on Pete anyway," Thelma replied. Then she leaned over and whispered something to Dorothy that I didn't hear.

They both laughed, low guttural laughs and then looked in my direction.

"Jane, you finished setting up?" Dorothy asked.

"Yes," I answered.

"You can take a break if you want to," Dorothy told me.

"Thanks."

Reluctantly, I left the dining room and headed toward the kitchen. If I wanted to eat, I would either have to do it now or wait until after they stopped serving the golden-agers.

Marjorie was the other permanent waitress, and she was sitting in the kitchen with two of the teenage busboys.

"Hungry?" she asked in a motherly voice.

"I guess so."

"Did you know that Billy is a classmate of my son's?" Marjorie questioned.

"Really?" I hadn't imagined that she had a teenage son though she looked to be a little older than Dorothy, maybe in her early forties. Marjorie was small and dark. Her last name was Flambé, both she and her husband were of French Canadian ancestry. I learned that many people in the area traced their roots from this background.

"My son Michael's fifteen," Marjorie told me.

"Really? It's hard to imagine you with a son that old," I said politely.

"Well, I wasn't much older than that when he was born. I was married though . . . And I may be old looking but I don't dye my hair like some I could mention."

That was a direct dig at Thelma, of course. At that point, I didn't understand what she objected to so much in Thelma.

Billy interrupted with his own view. "Thelma's not so bad."

I expected him to add 'for an old lady,' but he didn't.

When Marjorie left the kitchen, Billy said, "You know, I'm not in her son's class. I'm a senior. He's only a sophomore. We're on the soccer team together, maybe that's how she got confused."

I could see that he was trying to impress me with his maturity. I was having my own issues with maturity. A certain recent Dartmouth College graduate hadn't impressed me with his maturity either. Nonetheless, I listened to Billy with some interest. He confided, "I just broke up with my girlfriend. She was getting too serious. I want to do more with my life than most guys around here. I got plans."

"Like what?"

"I'm going to join the Coast Guard."

That struck me as funny. I know I shouldn't have, but I started to laugh. We were over a hundred miles from the ocean. My laugh was short but enough to hurt his feelings.

"I'm sorry," I tried to apologize. "I didn't mean to offend you."

He shrugged his shoulders as though he was used to my reaction or even worse.

"I love sailing. I sail with my granddad on Lake Champlain," he explained.

"Really. That's wonderful."

"Yes. I know the Coast Guard is different, but I want to get away from here as soon as I can."

Before he could continue, Dorothy and Thelma were on us. "Step lively," Dorothy told me harshly, "the oldsters are ready to chow down."

Thelma beckoned for Billy to follow her. He was busing her tables. Once work started, we had no time for anything else. I didn't even have time to think or examine what I was doing working as a waitress while my friends and former lovers were either relaxing on sunny beaches or starting their postgraduate careers.

After I had been working at the Fields for several weeks, I had to work breakfast. Dorothy was in a talkative mood and I took advantage of her good spirits, which I had learned were few and far between.

"Have you been married long?" I asked.

"Yes. Doug and I tied the knot seven years ago. Doug's my second. I got married when I got out of high school. He got killed in an accident while he was in the service."

"I'm so sorry."

"It was a long time ago. No kids. What about you?"

"Me? Well, at the moment I'm trying to sort out a lot of things about my life," I said vaguely and then added, "I just broke up with someone."

Thelma joined us after the breakfast crowd had cleared out. "What happened to Marjorie?"

"She's sick again," Dorothy grimaced.

"I bet she's pregnant," Thelma remarked in an unpleasant tone.

"You think Paul's still got it in him to make another baby?" Dorothy smirked.

They giggled like school girls. It was exclusive and excluding. They knew Marjorie's husband. Dorothy had gone to high school with Billy's mother. They were tied together by bonds as close as kinship.

"What you and Doug do this weekend?" Thelma asked.

"Nothing much," Dorothy answered in a shamefaced manner, "went up to the camp with my brother and his wife and kids."

I realized that the women didn't socialize much outside of work. I imagined it was because Dorothy was married and Thelma wasn't.

"I saw Sheridan. He was in town for a few days," Thelma told Dorothy.

"Doug saw him too. He told Doug he's moving to Alaska."

"Soon as the divorce is final and he can sell the house," Thelma added.

"What's Elaine going to do?" Dorothy asked.

"Move to Burlington with her folks. I'm going to miss Sheridan," Thelma said almost to herself.

Suddenly I realized how lonely Thelma must be. I wondered if her loneliness was anything like mine. I had said goodbye to someone just before I came to the Fields. It had hurt more than I had thought it would. Now I felt at loose ends. I was no longer in love with my art major and could not bear thinking of another year at Amberton without trips down to Dartmouth. Was it the same for Thelma or worse? She was stuck in a dead-end job in a tiny town where everyone knew her and her heartaches.

That night, when it was time to leave work, Thelma's car wouldn't start. I offered her a ride even though she lived in the opposite direction.

"Anyone still in the kitchen?" she asked.

"Billy," I told her.

"Maybe he has jumper cables and can start the damn thing," Thelma said.

"Will you be all right," I called after her.

"Sure. Billy will give me a ride, if he can't get my car going."

Without saying goodbye, she headed back toward the Inn.

I left and put her out of my mind. I had the next two days off. Susie called me from Switzerland. She was in love and might even marry or at least live with someone called Jean-Claude. She urged me to drop everything and join her in Europe. Europe was the place to be an artist, not tucked away in the quiet villages of New England. I listened to her as though she was on another planet. Still, the conversation with Susie unsettled me, and I puttered around the apartment the next day until I realized that I missed being with people.

Twenty miles west of the Fields, a small town was having a combination craft show and fair. I decided to drive over and see it. I took my camera with the hope that I would find something or someone of interest to photograph and later paint. The highlight of the fair was the flight of hot air balloons. It was such a beautiful summer day. The fair was a large one with numerous potters, weavers, and other artisans. There was a contest for the largest zucchini squash, which was won by a ten-year-old with a thirteen pounder. Girls and boys in shorts walked arm in arm through the various stands and stalls. The balloonists made elaborate preparations for their flights, while children and adults gazed longingly at the grownup toys. After numerous delays, they made ready for their flight and took off. The balloons were brightly colored — reds, oranges, purples, and greens. The balloonists were tanned men who seemed to look with disdain on those who dared only to observe and not participate. I shot several rolls of film hoping to get something I could paint from them.

As I reloaded my camera to take more pictures of the balloons sailing off into the distance, I noticed across the open field the sight of two familiar figures. There was Thelma and Billy arm in arm. She had her hair tied down with a scarf. Her attire was shorts and a midriff blouse that made her look like a teenager. Only her face betrayed her age, but I doubt if anyone else noticed. Billy looked lean, tall, and handsome. People were busy enjoying the day, relishing the warm sun and storing up the summer to keep them alive through the long harsh winter that lay somewhere beyond the sun. I felt embarrassed at seeing their intimacy. I watched them like a thief. There was a look of superiority or conceit on his face. She looked calm and genuinely happy. They never saw me. They didn't see anyone. They were too caught up in themselves as a couple.

When I returned to work, Dorothy was in one of her blackest moods. She had had to work the weekend.

"You're going to have to work Thelma's station. She isn't here today."

"Okay," I replied. I knew it was best not to ask any questions.

"Thelma knows better than to pull a stunt like this on me," Dorothy muttered to herself when she thought I couldn't hear her.

Luckily, it was a light day. The Inn was between bus tours. Marjorie came over to me when Dorothy was on her break.

"What's up?"

"Thelma's sick," I replied.

"I doubt it. She goes on these benders like. I don't mean she drinks. She was counting on Sheridan to marry her, and he left her flat. She's been dumped so many times that she just goes on a bender — she finds herself another guy and shacks up for a while. Always comes back, though. Keeps quiet for a while, then something happens and she goes on another one of her benders."

"Why does she keep getting left flat?" I questioned.

"Had a rough break in high school. She was in a snowmobile accident. One of the guys died. She lived, but it left her so she couldn't have kids. I guess none of the guys around here want you if you can't have kids."

"Everyone knows?"

"Sure. It's a small town and people talk."

In dismay, I blurted out, "Why doesn't she leave this town

then?"

"She did leave once. Came back about four years ago and took care of her folks till they died. I guess she doesn't have any place but this. This is her home, so she stays."

Marjorie believed she had told me everything I needed to know to understand. I didn't understand; however, I needed time to learn how few real choices in life any of us have.

She was right, Thelma didn't show up for three days and neither did Billy. Dorothy moped around and snapped at everybody all day. She never mentioned Thelma or her absence, however. On the fourth day, Marjorie told me that Billy's parents were going to notify the police even though he was seventeen. No one knew where they were. No one knew where to begin to search for Thelma or Billy, but without my saying a word, everyone knew they were together. I was working all of Thelma's shifts and extremely exhausted when Susie called me at four in the morning to say that the bloom of romance had faded with Jean-Claude because he wanted to live together in the good old United States and not Europe. Now Susie needed her trusted friend to console her. She would pay my way. Sleepily, I agreed. I had to give the Inn two weeks' notice and begged Susie to stay out of trouble until I got there.

The next day they returned. Billy stayed only long enough to collect his pay and turn in his uniform. No action was taken against Thelma. She was just back. Somehow I had expected her to be battered and worn, the way an alcoholic is after a weeklong bender. Instead, she was slightly tanned and, in a quiet way, happy. I overheard her talking to Dorothy shortly after we closed the dining room. It sounded so simple, the way things never are supposed to be. All she said, or at least all I heard her say, was, "We went to the seaside. Neither of us had ever seen it."

Two weeks later I was winging my way to Europe to visit my wealthy, confused friend. On to another life, another world — or at least so I thought at the time.

Indian Summer

Professor Eleanor Flowers sat in her office in the Buckman Building at Amberton College. Autumn was her favorite season. Nothing suited her more than to don a pair of walking shoes and her tweed wool jacket to go among the leaves and follow the well-worn paths that surrounded the campus of this New England college. She had chosen Amberton for its peaceful locale. She needed the subdued atmosphere in order to live a quiet peaceful life. In the years she had been at Amberton, she was able to finish her book of critical essays on the stories of the New England writer Sarah Orne Jewett, thus bringing her one step closer to gaining tenure.

With a combination of envy and apprehension, Professor Flowers watched the students crossing the quadrangle kick up the multicolored fallen leaves. Envy — because her college years were spent in a far different place. Apprehension — because she faced the possibility of leaving this place of security and beauty that had been her home for years. Her new book on women poets of the region was not coming along well. She had little difficulty doing the research, she was just having a problem getting her words on paper. She basically attributed her writer's block to another problem.

She had been saddled with a special section of Freshman English that was almost entirely composed of Native American students. These students had been recruited and sponsored under an endowment established by the estate of an early graduate of the college who went west to teach at an Indian mission school. When oil was discovered on the land that was given to her by the United States government, though it was within the reservation, she obtained all the oil rights and became a wealthy woman. Many people believed that all the riches should have belonged to the Indians; but be that as it may, she never shared the wealth with them. Instead, Millicent Buckman, the spinster schoolteacher, gave much of her fortune to Amberton College. The English Department was housed in the Buckman Building, and her estate established an endowment for the education of Indians at Amberton College, which was then an all-women's college. For nearly fifty years no Indians came East to avail themselves of these generous scholarships. In fact, few people knew about this endowment. Now that the college had become coeducational, Native Americans were becoming a recognizable minority on its campus.

Jonathan Deerhorn, the student she was awaiting, was one of the better Native American students. He had attended the famous Indian Academy, or as it was now called Native American Academy. It was a boarding school far from his reservation. There, it had been said, he had distinguished himself in science and math. Those were not Professor Flowers' subjects; she was a teacher of literature. On her desk was the final draft of a paper he handed in to her a few days before. It was supposed to be on Thoreau's essay "On Civil Disobedience." Since she had begun to teach this class, she had come to expect a certain amount of vagueness, confusion, and even poor grammar, but not what Jonathan Deerhorn produced. In insolently clear writing, he stated, I can't relate to this dude who wants to be free to disobey the laws of his tribe and who feels no responsibility for anyone but himself.

Eleanor Flowers was filled with despair as she looked at his paper and cringed as she recalled her conversation with the head of the department a few days earlier. Bill Harrison's message had been quite clear, and she felt the foreboding still.

"Ellie, I'm so disappointed. I thought you'd be able to handle this. In the last couple of years, we've been given a lot of flack about adding women to our team. Affirmative Action and all that. Though I've never understood all the fuss really. All this talk about power is beyond me. Everyone knows none of us in the academic world has any power."

"I know all of that, Dr. Harrison," Professor Flowers interrupted.

"Ellie," he continued and leaned forward across his desk. "This Indian, I mean, Native American endowment is very important to the college. We are very committed to giving them a true Amberton education. I thought you could handle these students with compassion and insight."

She wanted to tell him about all the students' lack of basic English skills and Jonathan Deerhorn's comment on his paper. She knew he wouldn't listen to her.

"You come up for tenure this spring, don't you Ellie? Well, it is always important to remember that publishing isn't enough, one must be a good teacher, as well."

She had nodded her head in agreement. She sat frozen in her seat as he continued to ramble on about other departmental concerns. For the first time, she began to evaluate her chances for tenure, and they looked gloomy. She knew that she was not well liked by her colleagues. The women, most of them feminists, resented her for not joining with them in the Women's Faculty Caucus, and the men eyed her with distrust and uncertainty.

The thought of leaving Amberton filled her with overwhelming sadness. She had sacrificed everything to get where she was and the thought of leaving was unbearable. She acknowledged no other life except the academic one. Where would she go, she wondered? She could not imagine returning to her hometown. There she had been an entirely different person, even her name had been different. Elena Maria Kwaitek, daughter of an immigrant factory worker with dirt under his fingernails and the smell of stale beer on his breath. She had been a slight blond girl with a quiet voice and weak blue eyes hidden behind thick glasses. She and her mother were the only women in a house filled with loud and often drunken men — her father and four brothers.

Her first escape had been going away to a convent boarding

school in the eastern part of the state. At Sacred Heart Academy, Sister Immaculata had asked her if her Polish last name meant anything, and she had replied, "Yes, Sister, it means flowers." She really wasn't sure if it meant that or sugar, but it was unimportant; after that she had decided to call herself Eleanor Flowers.

There she had learned to appreciate art, poetry, and beautiful things, as well as the pursuit of knowledge. The nuns were taken with her and wanted her to join the order.

"Sister Immaculata, I am unsure if I have a vocation," she lied. She barely believed in God, but she wanted the further education the sister offered. She wasn't sure whether she had received the scholarship because the nuns believed she would enter the convent or because she had the most qualifications. It didn't matter because by the time she finished college, she had lost her faith and won a fellowship to graduate school at the state university.

She might have maintained her connection with her family, at least before her mother died or even after on a superficial level except for one event. It happened during summer break after her first year in college. Professor Flowers never wanted to think about what happened and tried to bury it away. This horrible thing was a part of Elena Maria Kwaitek, not Professor Eleanor Flowers. Recently, in brilliant flashes the sight, smell, and feel of the boy her brother Mike introduced her to had been coming back to her. She felt herself pinned under him and the quick and painful act that followed. It was her first and only time. That wasn't the horror. What was etched into her memory was the next morning at breakfast when her brothers joked about what had happened to her the night before as though they had planned it.

"Do you know Elena has changed her name? Calls herself Flowers or something. Well, I guess she can't be a nun now. Frank fixed that," her brother Mike sneered.

"Yeah," her oldest brother Bryan agreed. They sniggered and poked at each other. Her mother questioned them, but they wouldn't explain to her. Eleanor Flowers went upstairs, packed her suitcase, and left the house only to return for her mother's funeral years later. She would call her mother once or twice a year. She didn't even return for her father's funeral. Elena Maria Kwaitek didn't exist anymore, except lately, her ghost was haunting Professor Flowers. She had wanted to live in a world where everyone was literate and poetic. At Amberton, she had found a place almost as perfect as her dreams.

Jonathan Deerhorn was prompt arriving at her office at exactly 3:30. He was carrying his text, a notebook, and had an earnest look of determination about him.

"Good afternoon, Professor Flowers," he said.

"Good afternoon, Jonathan."

He seated himself in the chair by her desk. He was relieved to discover the chair was placed in such a way that he could appear to be looking at her but in fact could gaze out the window instead. He had a hard time looking into people's eyes. For his people this was a sign of rudeness anyway. However, they (her people) believed it showed honesty and strength of character to be able to look directly into someone's eyes. He didn't understand that. It had been his experience that a liar found it easy to lie and someone who wasn't a liar could not do so, no matter where he focused his eyes.

She reminded him of a faded picture, as though she would eventually fade and blend into the light-colored walls. Her blouse was some lifeless pale color, and so was her hair, eyebrows, and eyelashes. He imagined that in the great whiteness of winter she could easily be lost. He wondered about the winter: Would he be able to stand it? He had been told that it stretched out long and unending for almost half the year.

"Jonathan," she said interrupting his thoughts, "Have you worked on a more appropriate response to the question concerning the Thoreau essay?"

"No, ma'am . . . No, Professor Flowers," he replied.

Some of the other Native American students believed that they had been given a woman teacher to humiliate them. He was not sure if that was true because as he looked around her office, he saw the same diplomas on her walls as he had seen on walls of his male professors. One thing he thought in her favor, she was not a faculty wife, but had made it on her own.

Professor Flowers sighed noticeably. The situation seemed hopeless to her. She would have to fail him and by doing so lose her chance for tenure. She spoke to him in as kind a voice as she could muster, "As you know, your theme was unacceptable. You have to do something in order to pass the next quarter."

She smiled weakly at him and added, "Naturally, I will try to help you as much as possible."

She hoped that she could convince both of them of the sincerity of that statement.

"I couldn't relate to Thoreau," Jonathan explained.

"Well, I'm afraid sometimes we have to . . . " she started.

Before she could continue, he interrupted, "To tell the truth, I didn't read the essay."

For a moment they sat in silent embarrassment gazing out the window at the sunny fall day.

In an attempt to find some common ground from which to proceed, "It's really beautiful this time of year," she said.

"Yeah, I guess it's okay," he agreed in a puzzled voice. He hadn't expected the conference to go this way.

"Do you know that they call this Indian summer?" she asked him.

"No," he answered.

"I'm not sure why it's called that. Perhaps it's because this good weather tricks us into believing that the long dark winter will never come."

She flushed noticeably when it occurred to her that somehow there was something derogatory in what she had said.

"Perhaps, tricked is the wrong word. Maybe it's better to say that this is an enchanted time of beautiful warm weather given to us to prepare for the long hard winter ahead."

"You don't like winter?" Jonathan questioned.

"That's not the point," she sighed.

"I thought all of you liked the cold and the snow," he continued, unaware that he might have said something to offend her.

She looked at him for the first time and realized that instead of the militant anger she had expected to find on his face, all she saw was the wistful sadness of adolescence.

"I suppose you're homesick," she said awkwardly, venturing forward on uneasy ground for she was not one to get too personal with her students. Conferences were a trial for that reason, because it forced her to deal with students one on one.

Jonathan Deerhorn stiffened at the sound of the tenderness in her voice.

"I've been away from home before," he responded quickly.

"Of course, but not so far away, I imagine, nor in such a foreign environment."

"There are others from my tribe here. I like lacrosse . . . also Native American House is a good place to live."

"Certainly," she said.

He had his pride, much like she had had all those years before when she entered the convent school. She had never let them see her cry or acknowledge the pain and loneliness she felt being away from the one person who had loved her — her blessed and saintly mother. And later, when she returned to college after that horrible summer, she willed herself to forget her violation.

"Jonathan, we must do something about your theme. It's too late to redo that paper. Instead, I want you to select another essay from the text and analyze it in a paper. Do you understand?"

"Yes, Professor Flowers. Thank you for your help."

He left quickly. It had been a strange interview as far as he was concerned. He had expected her to chew him out for not doing the assignment. He wasn't certain what he was going to do. He was pretty sure he could get a paper to hand in when the time came, but then again he had had a paper on the Thoreau essay that someone in Native American House had gotten an A on from another professor.

All he had to do was copy it over and hand it in to Professor Flowers. He just had never gotten around to doing it. It had turned cold now that the sun had gone down. Jonathan pulled up the collar of his denim jacket but didn't button it as he headed across the green. He thought about the long march (the Trail of Tears), his ancestors had made from the East to Oklahoma and supposed it was as cold and unforgiving for them as it promised to be for him. Maybe he should head for home too.

Nothing remained on the ground except dull dead leaves, and the cold air was heavy with the feeling of snow, when Professor Flowers walked toward her office for another conference with Jonathan Deerhorn. In the month since she had seen him, she had eaten and slept little, her writing lay neglected on her desk. She was plagued by recurring nightmares, paralyzed with fear, and discouraged by her failure with her student Jonathan, even though some of the other students had come around and were now doing passing work. Jonathan had even stopped coming to class. She had summoned him to her office for a confrontation.

It was a quarter after two when she reached her office. Jonathan was due there at three. While she waited, she tried to get into the notes for her New England women poets. Her notes seemed like the scribbling of a stranger. In despair she put them into her desk. As she did that, she noticed something from her past that she had kept with her through all her travels; it was a painted blown egg that her mother had decorated for her. Eleanor Flowers had never been sure why she had kept the egg, except as one of the few remembrances she had of her past. Now as she looked at the swirls of color and the intricate brilliant design, she realized that it was a precious, delicate thing of beauty, just like all the things she had taught herself to cherish and admire. It differed only because it had come out of her painful past.

The library clock chimed and brought back the reason for her being in her office. She gazed out the window and watched the students crossing the barren cold quadrangle. They were huddled in their coats, rushing quickly to escape the cold. Something told her that Jonathan Deerhorn was not coming, so she decided to go to him.

As she entered the Native American House, a mural of various Indians in different types of dress and wearing different kinds of headgear greeted her, A Native American coed sat at a desk in the lobby.

"May I help you?" she asked in a languid voice, barely lifting her dark eyes from the book she was reading.

"Yes, I would like to speak to Jonathan Deerhorn," Professor Flowers said.

"Did you say Jon Deerhorn? Jon's not here . . . He went home. He just couldn't hack it anymore."

"I see . . . Thank you," Eleanor Flowers said.

The professor scurried away. All was lost now. She would never get tenure or finish her book on New England women poets. Maybe it would have been better to have stayed in the house with her brothers, married one of the boys her brothers chose for her, or even become a nun. It was hopeless to try to hold on to anything that was beautiful and fragile. It slipped away like the beauty of a brief Indian summer day.

Hurriedly, she walked out of the building. She felt completely defeated. She didn't think about the other students who were passing, only about Jonathan Deerhorn. He had betrayed her, but then she had betrayed something or someone in her past as well. Eleanor Flowers wept for that and for what was lost forever.

Instead of walking back across the quadrangle, Professor Eleanor Flowers headed toward the jogger's path. It was quite cold and growing dark rapidly. She did not stroll leisurely but pressed on feverishly, as though pursued by some unspeakable terror. When she reached the point along the trail where she would have normally turned back, the light had almost faded completely and snow had begun to fall lightly. For a moment she stopped, then left the trail and proceeded on farther into the woods, leaving the college and everything she valued and believed lost behind her.

Starting From Different Place

I'm skipping school today. I deserve it. I'm a senior and there's exactly five and a half weeks of school left. Also, I have already been accepted at Dartmouth, Brown, and, here at home — Amberton. I'm a straight "A" student and have no fears in that way. I find it hard to believe that any teacher will fail me even if I take off for a few days. I really need to stay home to sort out the events of this weekend and how I feel about my parents. The house takes on a different feeling when I'm alone. My mom is working at her studio and my brothers Terry and Quinn are at school. No one will be here until after six. That will give me plenty of time to put down the events of this weekend. The only thing that bothers me is that I lied to my mother and told her I was going to school. I hate to lie to her because we are always straight with each other.

Anyone looking at this weekend would say that it was incredible. My father and his twenty-five-year-old wife were here on a visit. My parents have been divorced for almost three years. For a time after the divorce my mother and I were seeing a psychiatrist and he explained my father to us. In the doctor's eyes, it was a typical case — a middle-aged college professor who became involved with a student because he was going through a particularly climatic time in his life. The psychiatrist, however, had no words of wisdom or comfort for either my mother or me. He did have lots of theories about my future relationships with men. In a private session he cautioned me not to seek male approval in a series of promiscuous relationships either with my peers or older men. Perhaps that's the reason that my only male friend — in fact, my only friend — is Shaine, my "out" gay classmate. We even intend to go to the prom together wearing matching tuxes with pink cummerbunds.

Anyway, when the alimony ran out, we stopped going to the psychiatrist. My mother got a grant to work on her painting and with the child support, I got new braces for my teeth.

It is hard to say that I missed my father since the divorce. My father has always been remote and unapproachable. Either he locked himself in his study at home or he spent long hours in his office at the college. I grew up knowing that his work was more important than any of us. As I head off to college, I wonder if some professor will use me the way my father used all of us, including Rona, the Amberton student he had an affair with and married. I am not like Rona though. I have lived through this family drama and I know better.

In all fairness, Rona was far from a siren. She was scholarly looking with her soft brown eyes and pensive face. The only thing the least flamboyant about her was her red hair. She looked like the kind of Amberton student that sits around strumming a guitar to her melancholy poetry. My mother once said that Rona wrote poetry, using a mocking tone that made me want to throw away all my own notebook of poetry and never write another line.

How could I have described Rona before I described my mother? It seems disloyal and a betrayal. It isn't. At first it appeared that Rona was the center of attention this weekend, maybe it was my mother. I guess in the final analysis, it was my father, as usual.

How best to describe my mother Janet. She is in her early forties and doesn't look it. She is one of those women who doesn't have to worry about her weight. Before this weekend, I would have said that my mother was an optimist with an infinite capacity for hope. Don't get me wrong, my mother isn't a mindless Pollyanna. She has her dark days too, and this weekend may have been the darkest.

It all started on Friday morning when I came downstairs to breakfast. My mother sat at the table in jeans and with a scarf tied around her short black hair. I expected her to look fresh and alert, ready to meet the challenges of the day as usual. Instead, when I looked into her eyes, I realized she had been crying.

"Your father called," she said.

"And he and Rona aren't coming up after all," I replied as I bit into a piece of toast.

"To the contrary, they'll be here at six as planned. He had something he wanted to tell me before they arrived. He wished me to pass it on to you and your brothers."

"Why can't he tell us himself?"

"Well, Kera, it's not your father's style. He just couldn't bring himself to spring it on you. He thought a few hours preparation might be appropriate. So, I'm left with the task. Kera, Rona is pregnant."

I could not respond.

"Kera, did you hear what I said?" she asked.

"But he told me he couldn't have any more children," I protested.

"Apparently that wasn't as finalized as we all were led to believe," my mother countered.

Suddenly all the calm and reserve disintegrated. Tears streamed down her face. She wilted, and I put my arms around her trembling shoulders. I was confused. Where was the confident woman I knew? Why was she crying? Did she still love him? Then, too, trying to comfort her made me unable to express or understand my own feelings.

"I can't tell Terry and Quinn," she said to my surprise. "I want you to tell them for me."

Unable to find any other emotion, I chose anger and yelled, "Tell them their father's a liar?"

"Kera, I'm counting on you. I need your help. Rona's pregnant, there's nothing we can do to change that. You'll have a new brother or sister. Things have changed now."

"I thought I already had a sister. Her name is Rona," I retorted.

"You're not helping, Kera. You see how I am. I don't want to break down in front of your brothers. You must tell them."

"He lied. He said he couldn't have any more children," I

repeated oblivious to her pleas.

I could tell she had no answers for me, so I let my anger spill over to her. "What was all that crap about us being so special because we were the only children he would ever have?"

"Kera, all I know is that your father called this morning and said that Rona was five months pregnant and they couldn't camp out at the lake this weekend. He wanted you children to know before you saw her. He was in a rush and couldn't talk."

How like my father, and how like my mother to accept it, I thought angrily. "Why do you think he lied about not being able to have any more children?"

"I don't know. Your father has ambivalent feelings about children. After you were born, he talked about not having any more. We waited six years before your brothers were born, and then the same thing happened. He said that children were too expensive, that he was too involved with his work, that we were too old."

"He said he had a vasectomy," I persisted.

"If he did, he must have had it reversed. They can do that now. How the hell do I know!"

"You were married to him."

"And now I'm not, Kera. Why don't you ask him?"

"Do you think he wants this new baby?" I asked. I sounded young, like my eleven- year-old brothers. I wanted to cry from anger and unhappiness.

"I don't know, honey. You should ask him. Kera, talk to him. Tell him how you feel."

Tears came to my eyes. In the past, I tried not to cry in front of my mother. Since the divorce, I hadn't wanted to be a burden. But just then I needed my mother to comfort me. Not just for this, but for all the rough times I had been going through. Even I know that I should have other friends besides Shaine and it would be nice to think that when I go off to college, I will meet people who enjoy the same things I do. My mother shouldn't be my only confidante.

When Rona and my father arrived at a quarter to seven, they

expected dinner. My mother and I made something for them. Terry and Quinn sat silently starring at Rona with hatred clearly imprinted on their twin faces. Once the boys were in bed, my mother, father, Rona, and I retired to the living room like grown-ups. My parents drank vodka and tonic and Rona and I had lemonade.

"Well, Kera, how's everything?" my father asked awkwardly.

"Okay."

"Thank you, Janet, for putting us up for the weekend," my father said turning to my mother. "Naturally, Rona's not up to camping in her condition."

"It's all right, Ethan, I'm going to sleep at my studio while you're here."

"Mom!" I exclaimed. She hadn't told me that she'd decided to do that. I'd be the adult in charge of the house this weekend. I wasn't up to it.

"I only stayed to help out with dinner and see how the boys reacted to you and Rona."

That made me explode, "What about me?" I asked her.

"Kera, I told you before, ask your father to explain it to you."

"Explain what? It's obvious Rona and I are going to have a baby. Kera, I . . . er . . . we hoped you'd be happy too."

"Why should it make me happy?" I asked.

"Well, it'll be your little sister or brother," he said.

"I already have two brothers and no one asked me if I wanted them."

"That's different. You were six when they were born."

"Look," my mother interrupted, "this is where I came in, and I'm going to say goodnight." She packed a bag and left.

A look of annoyance passed across my father's face as the three of us listened to the sound of the car starting up and driving off.

Almost to himself, he said, "Janet should have told me that she was taking off like that."

"Why?" Rona asked. "I think it was nice of her to let us have the house to ourselves," she added softly.

"Not exactly. After all, Terry and Quinn are still here and so is Kera."

He didn't look at me when he said that. When he did look my way, he asked in a sarcastic tone, "You're not going off somewhere too, are you?"

"I have no place to go, Dad," I replied.

It was only Friday and I wondered how I could get through Saturday and Sunday with them. While my father went off to the liquor cabinet in the living room to make himself a drink, Rona and I sat alone in the kitchen trying to avoid looking at each other.

"I suppose you've been accepted into college by now," Rona said in a tentative voice.

"Yes. Dartmouth, Brown, and Amberton. I'm going to stay here at Amberton. It's familiar ground. I can live at home after my freshman year."

"Are you sure that's what you want to do?" Rona inquired.

"Aside from everything else, I believe the days for all-women's institutions are numbered. I want to get the special kind of education one can get at a women's college before they disappear."

"I know what you mean. I've always gone to all-girls schools. I went to a Catholic girls high school before I came to Amberton."

My father came back into the kitchen carrying a drink.

"All this needs is a little ice, and it'll be a perfect vodka and tonic," he said. He walked toward the refrigerator. Rona and I didn't go on with the conversation. It struck me how we both had tensed up when he came back into the kitchen.

"What were you two talking about?" he questioned Rona without looking at me.

"Kera's decided to go to Amberton instead of Dartmouth or Brown," she informed him.

"What? You must be kidding. I think it's a mistake choosing a girls' college over Dartmouth or Brown," he said as he placed his drink on the table.

Neither Rona nor I spoke.

"I suppose this is your mother's idea," he said harshly.

"No, it's mine," I replied.

"Well, it makes it easier for me financially if you do go to Amberton, since I was a tenured professor here for years," he said almost to himself.

Rona got up from the table. "I'm tired, Ethan. I think I'll go up to bed," she interjected.

"It's the first bedroom on the right. It's all ready for you and Dad," I told her.

"Thank you, Kera. Good night."

My father nodded to his wife. He put down his drink on the kitchen table and sat down opposite me.

"Dad, can I ask you something?" I said with hesitation.

"What is it?" He sounded bored.

"Never mind." I was losing my nerve.

"No. Talk to me. What is it? Your mother can't understand the sexual mores of your generation?"

"No, it's nothing like that. I just can't understand the sexual mores of your generation."

"What do you mean?" my father asked.

"You told us that you couldn't have any other children and that's why we were so special to you."

"First of all, I certainly hope I don't have to explain the facts of life to you at this late date. Secondly, this is a very private and personal matter. I don't have to discuss this with you." he replied.

"No, I guess not. I'm just your daughter."

"Besides, I told your mother to explain."

"Explain what? That you betrayed us just like you betrayed her?" I said. I was so close to losing it completely.

In a strangely calm, quiet voice, he said, " You don't know what you're talking about, Kera. Don't become the ultimate cliché, a bitter self-centered adolescent."

"Look who's talking. Nobody is more selfish than you."

"Ha! That shows how much you know. Having a child at

my age—I'm nearly fifty—is anything but selfish. Kera, you're old enough to handle some hard truths. I don't want to say anything to turn you against your mother, but I think she has put some strange ideas into your head about me being an oppressive male chauvinist. I taught at Amberton, a woman's college, for years, for chrissake. I'm not the enemy!"

"Of course not. You only seduced one of the teaching assistants," I replied.

"Really, young lady! Don't talk about things you know nothing about!"

He picked up his drink and went off to bed, leaving me alone to clean up the kitchen.

Terry and Quinn woke me at seven-thirty; they had softball practice at eight and asked me to drive them. I told them that Mom had the car. They had to call a friend's mom and ask her to take them. None of us thought of asking our father to drive them. I turned over and went back to sleep. I woke up to the smell of bacon. I went downstairs expecting to see my mother; instead I found my father. At the sight of him making breakfast, I felt a sudden rush of tenderness. At least, I said to myself, he must love Rona enough to do this. Maybe he'll love her child more than he loves my brothers or me.

"I was starving to death, so I came down and made some breakfast. Rona is sleeping in this morning."

"She'll love it when she wakes up," I said.

"This is for me," he replied, "Oh, you can have some. Rona doesn't eat meat. She was a strict vegetarian but will eat some chicken and turkey now that she's pregnant."

"Oh, I see," was all I managed to say.

He had his breakfast of bacon and eggs, toast, and coffee. I had some toast and coffee. The coffee was superb.

Saturday afternoon was dismal and rainy. My mother picked up Terry and Quinn at softball practice and treated them to lunch at McDonald's. She brought them home for long enough to change clothes and then dropped them off at the movies with friends. Rona was resting upstairs, and my father drove over to Amberton to talk with some former colleagues. When my mother returned, she started to make lasagna for dinner. I told her about breakfast.

"Don't judge your father too harshly," she told me. "After all he is starting over. We were married for most of our adult lives. When we divorced, it was a mutual agreement, Rona wasn't the reason. Both of us wanted to start over. It's just that we started from different places."

"But he doesn't love her either," I protested like a hurt child.

"Kera, you don't know that. I look at her and think I was like that when we first married. I thought he was a genius. Yet, I had my own private dreams that had nothing to do with him. I am lucky to be able to see those dreams come true. I have my children and my art as well. But what was there for your father after a while? He had a tenured post at a good college, the respect of his colleagues. But what other mountains were there for him to conquer? And then there was the adoring loving young woman — Rona."

I could tell my mother had thought about what she said. And maybe she truly believed what she was saying, but it still didn't justify what my father had done to his family or what he had done to me. I was not only filled with rage at him, but at her for trying to explain it away.

After a few moments silence, my mother said, "Kera dear, it is time for you to start over too. You need to go out on your own. Don't stay here at Amberton."

"But I want to go to Amberton," I insisted.

"Why?" Before I could answer, she continued, "You feel that you have to take care of us. Your brothers and I will be all right. It's your time now! Go to Brown. Find a life there. Find out who you are."

I fell silent and so did she. After she finished preparing dinner, she took a shower, changed her clothes, and left.

Saturday night dinner was quiet. Rona had the lasagna even

though it had meat in it. After dinner, Terry and Quinn were picked up by a friend's mother and taken over to his house to watch TV and sleep over. Rona, my father, and I sat in the living room. My father had brought a book with him and read while Rona and I sat silently watching him. All of us went to bed early.

Sunday morning came and Rona asked to be driven to the Catholic church. My father was disagreeable and annoyed, but he took her anyway.

After he dropped her off, he returned and asked, "Where's your mother's studio?"

"Why?"

"I want to talk to her, and since she refuses to confront me like a mature adult, I'm going over there."

"I don't think you should do that," I told him.

"Kera, you don't understand. It seems to me that a girl your age should be more compassionate. Why don't you have your own interests to keep you occupied anyway?"

I supposed that was a good question, but I didn't like it coming from him.

"Are you going to tell me where your mother is?" he asked sharply.

"No."

"Kera, don't be ridiculous," he snapped.

The argument went nowhere. Finally, he had to leave to pick up Rona from church.

When they returned, he announced sullenly, "We've decided to leave now. I want to beat the Sunday traffic."

Before they left, my mother returned. She was smiling happily, the way she does when her work goes well. The mother I loved and looked up to had returned. She walked back into the house and I was glad to see her again.

"Leaving?" she asked lightly.

"Yes," my father replied. "Want to beat the traffic."

He packed the car and deposited Rona in the front seat. He

came up to me and stood for a while just staring at me.

"Kera, you look so much like your mother," he said solemnly.

"Do I?"

"Yes, very strong and invincible."

Before I could say anything, my mother inquired, "You'll be up for her graduation on the twelfth of June, won't you?"

"If she wants me to come," he said to her, not looking at me.

"Of course she wants you to come," she answered for me.

I watched my parents go out to the car together. I heard him tell her that he wanted to talk to her and that I had refused to tell him where she was. He told her he'd call her during the week.

And then my father and Rona were gone.

"Thank you," my mother said and hugged me.

Which brings me back full circle. This Monday morning, I couldn't face school and teachers. No matter what my father said or didn't say about having any more children, there will be a new baby. Things have changed for this family and like in the nursery rhyme— all the king's horses and all the king's men can't put us back together again. Come September I will be leaving. I'll go to Dartmouth, which is only forty-five minutes away from here. Away but not too far away. I guess this weekend was a commencement of sorts, the end of something and the beginning for all of us, especially me.

After Mira Mahou

In a moment I shall be in my element, reading, sparkling, but it's the time before I'm on stage that is so hard for me to get through. The time when there is no audience, when I am alone and the voices speak to me anyway. They are the voices of memory, recalling with shame and regret times gone forever. Lately, the voices continue even when I weave my magic with my own words. I have a tale to spin like Homer or some other blind poet. True, this is a minor venue — the common room of Amberton College library. It is filled with students and junior faculty. Are they here to listen to me because I am a poet or because I'm the wife of the chair of the department? Where's Bill. There he is. I have some shocks for you, my love. Where's my fellow writer, Joyce? I wish she was here too. Perhaps she'll come later with that insipid bore of a husband of hers. Where to begin? At the beginning, of course.

> I come to you after Mira Mahou
> wearing her blue beret on kinky hair
> dyed red
> to share your bed
> worn brown with colored bodies

Norma was born on the lower east side of Manhattan to first-generation immigrants. Bill is fidgeting as usual. He looks so tired. Will he care what secrets I reveal in these poems tonight or will he fall asleep before I'm done? I write poetry, I said to him when we first met. There was hesitation in my voice, but it vanished when I saw the smile of approval on his face. I also swim, I said too quickly afterward. I had to do that in those days. Twenty-five years ago. Bill and Billy. Billy was learning to swim too. He was not so fleet, not so fishlike in the water. Too fat. Too fat with pink sensitive skin. Little short pudgy fingers not good for a musician. I play the piano as well as write poetry, and, of course, swim. Norma, the accomplished child and young woman.

> After Mira Mahou come I
> to share your bed worn brown
> with colored bodies
> What fusion of my dusty soul
> with yours
> What dreams transformed

That girl was coughing. She sounded like she was choking to death. Everyone was watching me from chairs, from the floor. It reminded me of doing recitations for the family. Read, Norma, a voice would say. Play, Norma, a voice would say. Practice, Norma Jean. Practice makes perfect, Norma Jean. Was Marilyn Monroe's name actually Norma Jean too? That's a laugh. They say Marilyn killed herself. What a legacy, if a name can carry a legacy.

> After Mira Mahou come I
> to share your bed worn brown
> with colored bodies
> what dreams transformed
> from Greeklike passion
> with you are doomed

I think Bill is listening. Does he hear my revelations? Tiny electric shocks to his brain from Norma. It was raining that night. I told him you were not at home. His name was Charles and he was the new assistant professor. There was something exciting and sensual in his large brown eyes. He looked young enough to be a student. He reminded me of a painter all those years ago when I was a college freshman home for summer vacation. I wandered the Greenwich Village Art Show. He looked more like a jazz musician with his dark glasses and black turtleneck sweater. He had a neatly trimmed goatee and mustache. He was the first black man I had ever found attractive.

He called me "little girl" in a mocking, playful tone. I slept with him more to prove I wasn't a "little girl" than to show how liberal I was. We had a summer together. His studio was on Greater Jones Street, and there I saw his painting of Mira Mahou. When I saw her, I knew why he called me a girl. Mira Mahou was a woman. Now, all those years later as I flirted with Charles, I wondered if I was more of a woman than Mira Mahou. I still doubt it. Nothing happened between us.

> After Mira Mahou come I
> to share your bed worn brown
> with colored bodies
> would that I too in mindless
> soulless abandon could
> thrust myself against your manly shield
> and doing so be one
> with Mira and her dusty sisters
> Freed at last

Where are you going? Home, dammit! I looked for my small jet-black beaded purse, but that's not the one I brought to this faculty party. I tried to find my husband Bill. He had vanished as usual. Then I thought it was better not to look for him. Better not to go too far, too deep into shadows of this gathering. Just find whatever purse I brought with me, retrieve our car keys from the gigantic bowl on the table in the foyer, and drive home. Bill would have to find his own way home.

After Mira Mahou come I

to share your bed
worn brown with colored bodies
Impaled upon his sacrificial sepulcher
like some sea-tossed maid.
But Mira is strong black stuff

Charles came to the house for a party. He brought his wife. She was a therapist. Strangely, she and Joyce were friends. The two women talked and excluded everyone else. I talked with Charles. He was attentive and polite. He lit my cigarette and although I was the hostess, he freshened my drink. Did he find me attractive or was he trying to impress the chair's wife? That night I couldn't sleep. I looked over at Bill, and he looked dead. His face was so white and still and devoid of expression without his blue eyes staring out at me. Bill dead. Me dead. Billy is the only one dead. What must death be like? If it's not the cessation of everything, then what good is it? If pain continues, if consciousness goes on, what good is dying? Billy's bathing trunks washed away by the Caribbean. Billy's pink puffy little boy's face covered with snot and seaweed and scum from the water. His face was black and blue and his eyes bulged out of his head. Remembrance of the Island Paradise, my dead son. His naked body bruised and scarred for eternity. Is he bones by now? My God!

I come to you after Mira Mahou
to share your bed
worn brown with colored bodies
But Mira is strong black stuff
sure in her earthlike
guttural manipulations
not loving and hating
in one swollen heart

Anne and Damon and Bill and I that one time in bed together. All on the waterbed together. Trying to find a new meaning to life after the death of the Kennedys, Martin Luther King, Jr., and the Vietnam War. Now Damon and Anne are parted. Anne and I tried to hold on to each other. Soon she will be leaving. Is Bill interested in what I have to say after all these years? What does he care about? His dead son? His wife's infidelities? I wish my words, my thoughts were little electric shocks to his brain that could make him suffer. Suffer as I have. He never connected with his own son. At least I can't remember them together. Reconstruct them, Norma. You have an imagination. Bill and Billy. Mama and Daddy playing tennis together. Mama's fast, tanned legs. Mama's short white skirts whooshing by. Mama being faster and better than Daddy. Billy reading. Read, Billy! Read for Mama!

> But Mira is strong black stuff
> Sure in her
> earthlike guttural movements
> not loving and hating
> in one swollen heart
> the mud that oozes
> rich between her knowing toes

No more children. It was too late by then. It made me remember that the ones I had aborted could not be retrieved. Of course, I would have salvaged any of them regardless of color if I could have had one that was from my own body, but there was no hope. All I had now was the poetry, putting words on paper, stringing images together instead of the truth of life and love.

Joyce is here, after all. She's crying. Wonder what touched her so profoundly to make her cry. Perhaps she is just going mad again. Or was it my poetry that moved her so? The recitation of my petty sins, my minor heart laid bare for all to see? Norma's failure is not just her marriage, not that her poetry is minor and trivial, but that she lost her child. She had a child for nine years and let the precious being slip through her fingers like the foam on the tips of the waves.

I wonder, Mira Mahou. I wonder if your blackness gives you a greater tragedy than my own? Would that you were here tonight to hear this ode to you. My life seeps out of me year by year, and in a while all will be gone. Lost. Lost like my son. Bill has gotten up and is leaving. Why?

> After Mira Mahou come I
> damned white in this
> sooty citadel of my devouring flesh

Good Mother—Good Girl

My mother was born Lili Mae Anderson in rural South Carolina, the fourth of the ten children of Marcus Anderson and Rose of Sharon Titus. She was the first of three girls. All the girls went to college, my mother would say with pride. She didn't have equal pride for her brothers. All of them were gone from war and troubles long before I came into this world.

My mother was the prettiest of the sisters everyone said. Pretty because of her light skin with freckles, auburn-colored curly long hair, and hazel eyes.

She talked often about her sisters to me. "We were good girls." She would say, "Good in the old-fashioned way."

"I know, Mama," I'd answer.

"We were taught what was important — to get an education, to be ladies, to carry yourself with dignity, and not to give yourself to some no account fool."

I would nod my head obediently: I was a good girl too. My one aim in life to be a good daughter and make my mother proud of me.

My mother had come a long way from South Carolina by then. She had an advanced degree in Social Work and was a psychiatric social worker and part-time college professor in New York City. She also was married to her second husband, not to my father.

She had plans for me. To earn her love and respect, I had to be a good girl, and I was. I was always cheerful, helpful, and smart. I was my mother's good girl. I graduated at the head of my class. I got a Ph.D. at the age of twenty-four. The good girl who won every award, broke every record, and gave her mother top bragging rights. Except for one slip, one mistake, one transgression that changed everything forever.

"Are you sure you're pregnant?" my mother demanded.

I wanted to give her a smart comeback like — of course, I'm sure. I just successfully defended my doctoral dissertation, I should be able to figure this out. But I was too overwhelmed by my predicament to say anything. I began to cry. I had no idea what was going to happen to me. My mother put her arms around me and held me to her.

"I suppose it happened this summer on the Cape with that white actor," my mother said.

"Yes," I managed to reply. "What will happen to me? It's an impossible situation . . . " I began.

"Nothing is impossible," my mother interrupted with steely resolve in her voice. "I'll fix this," she said emphatically. And she did. That was my mother. That was me as a daughter. That was then.

This is now. This is me as a mother with Xanda, my pale beautiful daughter with her hazel green eyes and lovely smile. The night before she was to begin kindergarten, she was excited and I was sad. It seemed to me that her life was on fast forward and I wanted it to slow down, so that she'd stay my little baby awhile longer.

Added to the nightly ritual of her bath and brushing her teeth was the laying out of her first day of school clothes—a dark green corduroy jumper with a pale greenish-yellow turtleneck sweater, green socks, and much too expensive sneakers. I was allowed to do all of this. Then my daughter dismissed me saying, " I want Daddy to read to me."

"Are you sure?" I asked. I thought that on this special evening I should be allowed more privileges. Xanda had different ideas.

"I want Daddy to read to me like always," she replied.

I picked up her favorite book, Corduroy, and took it out to Charles who was stretched out on the couch in front of the television. Though the TV was on, he wasn't watching it.

My husband of nearly five years was in a funk that bordered on depression. Charles had been up for tenure at Amberton College, but he didn't get it. He could, however, remain at Amberton in a nontenured administrative position, as head of minority recruitment with the possibility of teaching a course of two. Since I wanted to stay in Dresden, that seemed an ideal solution to me. I did not work at Amberton, except as a consultant. I had a thriving private practice as a child psychologist, and Xanda was starting school at the fine small public school in town.

Charles was having none of it. He wanted tenure as a full professor, if not at Amberton, then somewhere else. He had dreams of moving South, working at one of the formerly all black colleges, establishing a life in what all the magazines were calling the New South. It was the way of the future for young African-Americans like us, he kept telling me.

When he realized that it wasn't as easy as that to convince me to make the move, he came up with a new plan. We would try teaching overseas on the international school circuit. All that weighed heavily on him as he lay stretched out on the couch.

"Xanda wants you to read to her," I said. I handed him the book.

He got up and headed toward our daughter's bedroom. "Daddy's coming," he called. He smiled. I followed him to the door of Xanda's room. I stood in the doorway as he sat down on her bed and began to read.

"Corduroy is a bear who once lived in the toy department . . ."

Gone was the anger and sadness that seemed to surround Charles in the weeks he had been dealing with this dilemma.

Xanda had the power to change his mood and make him happy. Something I was never able to do.

As I stood in the doorway and listened to Charles reading to Xanda, I envied them their closeness and ability to change each other's mood. I was unsure whether I envied Xanda's love for Charles or his love for her. Perhaps it was that I couldn't love either one of them without analyzing and questioning the relationship.

When Charles came to the end of the story, Xanda was almost

asleep.

"'You must be a friend,' said Corduroy. 'I've always wanted a friend,'" Charles read.

Then in a high falsetto voice, Charles read, "'Me too!'"

Xanda giggled sleepily. "Goodnight, Daddy," and added "Goodnight, Mommie."

She knew I had been standing there all the time. I asked myself why I hadn't joined them in the room. I had no answer. That was me as a mother.

One cold Dresden morning the phone rang. We were awaiting a phone call from Dr. Koppelmann from the Hague International School in the Netherlands. It wasn't him, it was my stepfather Ted.

"Darise, your mother's gone," he said. Gone, I thought. Where's she gone? Has she driven up to the house on the Cape? It's winter though. Isn't that strange? Mother's gone? Maybe she had gone down to South Carolina to visit her Aunt Sophie who is 92 years young. Mother's gone? Has she finally left you, Ted? Even though these thoughts rushed through my head, I remained silent.

"Aneurism," he explained. Of course, I knew what he meant. He meant my mother was dead. I was an orphan. I was a daughter without a mother. I was lost.

Ted did most of the talking, which was unusual for him. There would be a memorial service in New York, and she would be buried in South Carolina in the family plot. Ted sounded so apologetic about making arrangements without me. I was the daughter, but he was the husband. He had been the husband for seventeen years. My great aunt asked me who made the arrangements, and when I told her Ted did, she clucked her tongue and said, "But you're the daughter." I nodded and remained silent. I didn't tell her that I couldn't have made the arrangements. Just because I had a Ph.D. in psychology, it didn't mean I was equipped to bury my mother. I could barely pick out what I was going to wear or what Xanda, my five-year-old daughter, was going to wear.

It never occurred to me to question whether Charles was going with us to New York and then on to South Carolina.

"I can only accompany you to New York. Do you want Xanda to go with you all the way to South Carolina or come back to Dresden with me?" Charles asked.

I had no answer for Charles. I hadn't actually thought things out. For example, even though I'm a child psychologist, I hadn't thought about my five-year-old daughter and her reaction to her grandmother's death. I know about children and grieving. But what I was more concerned about was Xanda seeing me grieve. There was no way to avoid that. I couldn't make those kind of decisions. I wanted to be alone in my grief. I wanted to shut myself up in my room and sleep. I wanted someone to fix me meals and leave them outside my door. I thought if I lived like that for about a month, the worst would be over and I would emerge, free of pain and sadness. Then I would resume my life with a new status. Only then would I be able to make decisions and arrangements.

Doing what was best for Xanda was impossible for me to determine, and it angered me that Charles kept insisting that I decide. I screamed at him and he left me alone. Xanda threw enough clothes in her suitcase to stay away for a month. After she went to bed, I repacked her bag. She had packed her favorite items — a pair of panties with strawberries on them, her pink socks with ruffles, two pairs of shorts even though it was February. She had packed her I Luv New York T-shirt that her grandmother had bought for her. I decided to leave it in the suitcase.

When she unpacked, she wondered if her Grannie would be able to see the T-shirt when she wore it.

I knew shorts and a T-shirt were inappropriate attire for a funeral, so I put a navy blue velveteen dress with a white lace collar and cuffs in the suitcase. Though I don't believe in such things, I felt like my mother was guiding and directing me as I filled my daughter's suitcase. Take out the pink socks and put in the white ones, my mother's voice told me. Then she helped me to pack my own bag.

I was surprised that Charles didn't want to drive to New York

City. We flew.

"From the way you packed, I see you are taking Xanda with you down South," Charles said.

He seemed disappointed.

"I called Joyce," he said. "She said that she would help with Xanda. She could pick her up from school." His mention of Joyce, my best friend in Dresden, embarrassed me. I hadn't thought to call her. That was a sign of how confused and unsettled I was.

"It'll be okay," I told him. I wasn't sure why but it seemed important that Xanda go with me all the way. I needed her to remind me that beyond the services in New York and the burial in South Carolina, that there was a place called Dresden, a life to be lived and a tomorrow that called for me to be a responsible adult and a mother.

Charles was silent for the rest of the trip to New York.

However, when we got to the city, Charles pitched in with my stepfather and handled everything. That was fine with me. I had no decisions to make, and if I did, I asked their advice and went with whatever they suggested. My biggest challenge was to explain all of this to Xanda. The apartment that she had visited many times was still so full of her grandmother, yet she was absent.

"Will Grannie have any more birthdays?" Xanda wondered because they shared the same birthday.

"Grannie won't get any older, but we can remember her birthday just the same.

"Will I be as old as Grannie?"

I replied that before she got to be that old, I would be that age. I regretted saying it as soon as it was out of my mouth. I knew that when children experienced the death of someone close to them, they worried about the loss of their own parents; and that Xanda would make that leap of thought too.

Instead she said, "But you're already older than Grannie,"

Incredulous, I argued with her, "Your Grannie was my mother, so she had to be older."

"But Grannie always called you Old Lady."

The name she called me was Old Lady Loose Tooth. It came from a time when I was a year or so older than Xanda and had lost one of my two front teeth and the other was hanging precariously. I refused to let my mother take it out. I remembered weeping at my fate, believing that I would be toothless forever.

"Old Lady Loose Tooth," my mother said, "I'll love you no matter how bad you look."

I got my adult teeth, but the name stuck, and in time became abbreviated to Old Lady. It was the truth of things, I told myself, that I was as far from being an old lady then as I was from feeling like an adult now.

Right after the New York City memorial services, Charles flew back to Dresden leaving Xanda and me to continue the journey to bury my mother. One of the last acts that was forced on me by my stepfather was to clear away the papers on my mother's desk.

"These are personal papers," Ted said. "Of course, I took care of the bills and financial things." It was strange to see how their marriage worked. Despite my mother's solid independence, they were clearly a team. On the other hand, Charles and I had individual checking accounts. We alternated paying bills from each account on a monthly basis.

Amongst her papers in her day planner was a ticket stub to a Broadway play, a playbill, and an unfinished letter to the star of the play Karl Alan Hewitt. The striking, chiseled face of Karl Alan Hewitt as a World War Two officer startled me. He hadn't changed. His blue/green eyes seemed to stare intently at me from the playbill. I wondered what my mother was trying to do. Had she intended to make a correction on the solution she had made years before. Reluctantly, I read the letter.

Dear Karl,

It seems unbelievable that I should hesitate to use your first name, especially since what I am going to tell you is of a truly intimate nature. Let me quickly assure you this isn't an attempt to extort money from you or grab 15 minutes of fame.

We met about six years ago on the Cape through my daughter Darise. For a brief time you were quite taken with Darise, and she was quite taken with you. Then came your unfortunate automobile accident and your move to the West Coast. You never, as far as I know, got in contact with my daughter. We both assumed you had no desire to see her again, and I convinced her despite the outcome of your brief relationship that it was best she not contact you. She listened to her mother.

Let me quickly tell you that my daughter doesn't know I'm writing you now. I'm not sure she would approve. I have decided that you should know that the two of you produced a child . . .

The letter ended there. Perhaps if I wasn't on tranquilizers, I would have flown into a rage at my mother's presumption. I'm not sure my daughter would approve she had written. My mother knew damn well I wouldn't approve. I didn't want Karl to know. Charles is the only father that Xanda has ever known and, as far as I am concerned, is the only father she needs. My mother adored Charles. What made my mother change her mind about Charles? Was it that he didn't get tenure at Amberton? Was it that he intended to take us across the world? Did she think I would go? Now she was gone, and I had to make my own decisions.

I shuddered when I thought that if she had accomplished what she had intended, it would have put in motion things that would not only change Xanda's, Charles's, and my life, but Karl Hewitt's as well. My mother thought that as my mother she had the privilege to make that earth-shattering decision. Now it was my time to make the decision.

I stuffed the playbill and the half-finished letter in my suitcase. I took everything with me to South Carolina and then back to Dresden.

Xanda's first plane ride had been the trip to New York, and the second one was the trip back to Dresden from South Carolina.

"Are you glad to be going home?" I asked my daughter.

"Yes, Mommie. I can't wait to see Daddy." She hesitated and asked, "You'll be glad to see Daddy too, won't you Mommie?"

"Of course, darling."

Though I was still in the world of grief and sadness, I could feel myself emerging slowly with one certainty. Now that I had ceased to be a daughter, I was at last in a position to be a good mother.

I wondered if Charles would be glad to see us. Wondered if he expected us to leave Dresden and go off with him to the Hague or some other faraway place. I promised myself I would tell Xanda about Karl Hewitt when the time came. Right now, I am the mother and I make the decision. Dresden is where we belong. It is the place where I can keep my daughter safe and allow her to grow.

Burning or Coming Down

The new summerhouse is on the lake. It still smells of raw wood and paint. I have a good feeling about it. The lake is surrounded by houses, mostly A-frames that look like they have been cut out of a gigantic puzzle. Moored in front of each house is some kind of boat. We have brought our boat with us. No one really swims very much in this part of the lake anymore. People still do a vague sort of fishing there. Mostly people come here because it is far away from New York and Boston and they still have the illusion that they are in some kind of primitive society. But Dresden and its Amberton is only a brief car ride away, and one can retreat to that bastion of academic civilization whenever necessary. Peter and I could never exist far from the arena in which we have spent most of our lives.

We haven't spoken to each other for several hours since somewhere outside of Boston when we had a quarrel. It wasn't serious as arguments go. I can remember one night we quarreled about whose turn it was to call Kentucky Fried Chicken. Now Peter is driving stone-faced and silent while I pretend to sleep. I am discovering that I pretend to be asleep a lot. It is not the quarrel that makes me turn off, but my need to shut Peter out of my consciousness. I don't really care what my brilliant young husband's views are on politics or women's liberation. I know his ideas. They are old, and I am tired of them. Even the most original or unusual of his complaints no longer interest me.

One night, for instance, he said, "There's sand in the bed." I pretended to be asleep but I wanted to say to him, "So turn on your lamp and enjoy the beach." I didn't say that. I watched while he turned on the light and pulled back the covers to search for sand. Ridiculous? True, nonetheless. And after that, a three o'clock discussion on which of us was mentally unbalanced. In the midst of that, I found myself thinking that I was because I had listened to him. I felt stupid and old and missed never truly being young. The only thing of consequence in my life at that moment was the fact that I was nearly finished with my dissertation. Besides, Peter was totally and completely without an imagination and/or fantasy life. That, of course, was when he said it.

"Gwennie, I've been wanting to talk to you about this for some time, but I just couldn't. I have been trying to work things out on my own because I didn't want to hassle you while you were doing your dissertation. I know how rough that can be. But you and I haven't been communicating lately, and I have to talk to you."

Peter sat up in bed on that note. I noticed for the first time that he wasn't wearing a pajama top. I appreciated his thirty-year old body in an objective sort of way. We had been married for ten years and much of the mystery had worn thin. What I did notice with some interest were lines of worry and trouble on his face that made it look almost tortured.

"I have been having an affair with Sandy," he blurted out swiftly.

There was a proper response that I managed to give after a moment. I slapped his face and started to cry. I got out of our bed.

"What are you going to do?" he asked.

"Leave you . . . You bastard!"

I pulled out a suitcase and started throwing things in it. I remember distinctly putting every bra I owned in it. It was only an overnight bag and suddenly I felt foolish. I couldn't leave my husband without being a fool, I thought. I looked back at Peter and thought I saw a glimmer of amusement on his face. I did the only thing I knew I could do. I went into the study and started to burn my thesis. He ran to me. He grabbed my hands and pulled me away.

"You're hysterical. You don't know what you're doing," he said.

"Yes, I do. I hate it. I hate it," I cried. Visions of Sandy—soft curves, full bosomed, warm thighs came to me. What would she burn?

"It's over," he added when he had put out the fire.

I found myself back in bed with the smell of burnt paper in my nostrils and a few blisters on my fingers. In a moment Peter had a cup of lukewarm tea next to me. The cup looked small and cheap. After ten years of marriage, if you don't have children, you should at least have cups that are china and not chipped earthenware.

"It's over," he repeated. He was shaking. I saw something in his face that I had only seen once before at his father's funeral. Grief was shining in his eyes.

"Peter, I don't want this," I said pushing the cup away from me. "Do we have any Scotch?"

"I think so."

He stumbled out of the bedroom. I heard him move around the apartment muttering to himself. I didn't think of love. I knew Peter well enough to know he wasn't in love with his undergraduate assistant. I was shocked that there was even passion in him. Shocked that he was not one with the Peruvian Indians he had been studying for years. I felt such defeat that he had spent himself on Sandy while I had saved myself up for my dissertation on the myth of success in the novels of Theodore Dreiser. Or was it still junior high school and because Peter had finished his project first, he was allowed to have fun? Time still hasn't clarified any of this.

"When was it over?" I asked him, the edge returning to my voice. He had made a weak and ineffectual drink.

There was a frightened little boy expression on his face and I knew that it wasn't really over. He had only told me that which might momentarily heal my pride.

"Not long," he answered in a timid voice. Where was the Peter who had stopped me from burning my dissertation? But then again, what did that have to do with love or passion or pretty students or marriage?

Suppose I had slashed my wrists, would he be here holding them until the doctor arrived? Could he manage that with those powerful hands and with his weak ineffectual heart?

"Does she know?"

"Of course, she knows. Gwen, you're not making sense. Trying to burn your thesis like that. Honestly, honey . . ."

"Peter, I have to get out of here for a while. I can't stay here."

I got out of bed and dressed. I didn't know where to go. I wished that I had a male friend into whose arms I could fall for the night. There was no one. I wound up at my brother's apartment in the Village. I slept in the living room on his couch and smelled the burlap wall covering all night.

Roy is forty, balding, and out of step with time and fashion, which belies all those myths about gays. Before he would let me sleep, he had to talk to me.

"Pete fooling around? I don't believe it."

"It's true. He confessed," I said bitterly.

"Relationships are hard, Gwen. I've been very unhappy at times and other times, I've been unbelievably happy. But I know one thing about life. Things have a way of working themselves out, for better or worse . . . Everything will be all right, Gwen. Pete loves you."

How funny for him to talk of love. It was not what I had been thinking of. I was angry at Peter's betrayal, not at his sharing himself with another woman. I wasn't sure then, nor am I sure now, what love is all about.

As we talked, Roy did the dishes. We talked about my life mostly. He told me how much he envied me my achievements in school. We never mentioned our parents and their rejection of him, though it was the underlying theme of our conversation. As I looked at him and at his overly quaint apartment, I wondered what tied us together. All I could see was that both of us had been wounded in life. Not severely, however, not tragically; but only cut slightly — a nick like a man gets when his razor is dull. Our souls had not been assassinated, only in my case, it seems to have been dulled or numbed to sensation. I felt tenderness for my brother for the first time because of that. We were closer now than we had been as children. Ten years separated us in age and school had been the most significant thing in my life before Peter. I had always believed that next to being beautiful, the most priceless quality for a woman to possess was brilliance.

However, I see my brilliance as being my undoing. When I met Peter at school, I had thrown myself into love like it was a course in which I had to get an A. The A, of course, was marriage. I woke up one day feeling that I had missed life by reading Shakespeare on my own instead of learning to dance, by writing poetry instead of going steady. And so when Peter came along, I saw him as a sign that I must develop myself as a human being. Both of us did in the beginning. He had only some very shoddy adolescent experiences with girls quite different from me, and I was an anachronism — a virgin. When I look back on it now—the walks we took, the time spent together in the library, making love in his room; it was indeed romantic and naively idyllic. Peter became the only person in my life. For years I told myself, he was all I needed.

There was one disturbing memory that I think sent me rushing to Peter. A teacher of mine named Frieda Arnold went berserk and ripped off her clothes in front of our class when I was a sophomore at an all-girls high school. She was near retirement age and her beloved mother had just died several months earlier. Her history was well known to the students. Frieda Arnold had graduated from high school at fifteen and finished college at nineteen. From there she had come to teach and grow old at our high school among the female students and faculty. Her bizarre behavior in the classroom had caused a minor stir for a while and even reached the newspapers. I listened with a frightened uneasy feeling as my classmates with their developing bosoms and rosy futures imprinted on their faces analyzed Frieda's problem. She had never been kissed, held, or loved. Her body was a vast wasted desert. This barren landscape of a woman had been smothered by her mother. It was reported that she called her mother at least twice a day and continued to be seen sitting in the telephone booth at the same time even after her mother had died. In the teacher's cafeteria, a friendly faculty member told us that

Miss Arnold kept to herself eating the lunch prepared for her by her mother and sipping the school milk like a lonely child.

All the teachers seemed as stricken by her outburst as the students were. Naturally, she was institutionalized and most of us tried to forget her. Just when she had settled into a comfortable place in the back of my mind, she came back to haunt me forever. Frieda Arnold drowned herself in the East River while still a patient in a mental hospital. Then came the nightmare visions of her virginal withered face, her shrunken loveless body, and I began to see the striking parallels of our lives. Visions of Frieda Arnold clouded my own sense of accomplishments as a scholar, so I accepted Peter. I accepted his love, his dingy airless room, and gave myself over to sex in hopes of assuaging madness.

It seemed natural to leave graduate school and go to work to support Peter while he finished his dissertation. It seemed good to plan budget meals, to go to discount student movies and concerts. It was good to go to bed in our tiny apartment and follow the rules of the sex manual we had purchased jointly. I didn't need anything except my doctorate to round out my life. Because of Roy, my family had welcomed Peter as a son and saw our marriage in the best possible light.

I slept badly on Roy's couch. In the morning, I made the coffee. Roy looked pale and worn, as though it was he and not I that had parted from his home, his spouse, and all he had believed secure.

"Gwen, what are you going to do?"

He looked unhappy. The thought flashed through my head that he might want me to leave.

"I don't know, Roy. I thought about it and Peter did say this thing is over with . . . We didn't really talk."

I didn't feel the way I sounded. There was great fury inside of me. At the same time I felt powerless to express my rage. I couldn't say it to Roy. "How's the coffee?" I asked, completely off the subject."

"Good . . . really good . . . How'd you make it? Mine's always bitter."

He seemed visibly relieved that I could cope. His face brightened, and he poured himself another cup of coffee. I felt sorry that I had come to him like this. After all, he needed things too and lived his life without bringing it down upon me. Roy hadn't had dinner with Peter and me in months because he knew I was working so hard on my dissertation. He deserved better than life had given him.

"Roy," I said, "thanks for everything. I'm going back home this morning. I think the only thing is to face Peter."

"Peter and you love each other," Roy answered.

"Is that so important?"

He looked puzzled and bewildered. "Of course it is."

I hadn't unpacked, so I was out of his apartment in a flash. I went home as I always knew I would.

Today we were going to seed the lawn and take the boat out, but it rained. It rained and rained and rained. Peter tried for a while not to open his briefcase with the notes for his new book. I tried to avoid talking. I polished my toenails instead. It is the first time I have done that since I was a girl at camp. Then I started one of the six books I brought with me. Tomorrow Peter will go to Dresden and buy some liquor so that we will have something to drink during the silences. Sandy is in Europe and engaged to an engineering student. My dissertation was accepted, and I begin teaching full time this fall. Nothing happened except on the way up here Peter and I got into a silly argument outside of Boston and didn't speak to each other until we got to our new summerhouse.

You see, it is very simple. I don't have the stuff necessary to fight with, and I am not sure if I know what I would be fighting for. There was a moment when I thought there might be some shining magic called love, some sultry perfumed dagger of passion; but anything like that faded before I could grasp it. Before I could master it with the chiseled skill of my intellect or let it overcome my frozen heart.

A Resident of Dresden

I Brown v. Board of Education

It all started when the Dresden Union High School asked me to speak to the students on the fiftieth anniversary of the Brown versus the Board of Education decision of the Supreme Court. Though most of the teachers were not old enough or informed enough to know that the purpose of the 1954 case was to end segregation of the races in schools, the school administration declared it should be commemorated as a sign of this New England college town's multicultural liberalism. And I was recognized as someone who had lived through those times and who also was a long-established resident of Dresden. Of course, the most important fact is that I'm African-American. I'm all right with that term since I never particularly liked the term black. We as a people are of such varied hues, it is hard for me to accept one blanket color designation. Growing up I remember being called colored, which to my mind is different from being "a person of color." Then, of course, Negro was the most acceptable term.

Trying to get my thoughts in order, I picked up a tape recorder and began to talk into it. (I have a tendency to go off on tangents.) This tape recorder is as high tech as I get. I don't own a computer or a cell phone. I just got an answering machine for my shop two years ago. The tape recorder is how I was able to compose the speech I gave to the high school students.

Standing behind the podium on the stage of Dresden Union High School, I delivered my speech.

"In the town where I came from in the South — there were

two high schools — one for whites and one for us. These schools were as different as night and day. Those African-American families who had serious hopes for their children and the financial means sent the children North for a high school education. The children often returned to the South to attend black colleges. Unfortunately, my family was not in any position to send any of us (we were ten children) North.

"After the Supreme Court Decision there were years of ugliness. In other parts of the South, the National Guard protected a few lone black students entering formerly whites-only schools. Lines of screaming, spitting white people attacked little children as they entered school buildings. The governor of one state stood in a doorway, barring the admittance of one lone African-American student, saying, "Segregation now, segregation forever." These are pictures seared into my memory. I was twelve years old when the Supreme Court desegregated schools.

"The fact is, the schools in my hometown were still segregated more than a decade later. It was only when the dilapidated school for blacks mysteriously burned to the ground that they tore down the white school and built a new school for everyone. When I knew I was going to speak to you here at Dresden Union High School, I called my nephew to ask about Carter Weston Memorial High School (the present high school in my hometown). He said that of the ten National Merit Scholarship winners, six were black. He said also that Weston Memorial High's predominantly black basketball and football teams were state champions. That's progress, of course. I imagine that seems remote to all of you. So, I want to speak of things I think that reach across the years and have an impact here in Dresden, as well as, the rest of the world.

"For example, out of the Civil Rights movement came great people like Martin Luther King, Jr., and a new way of looking at things. As I stand before you, I try to imagine this same gathering in this same place 50 years ago or even 100 years ago. Today there is diversity — not just color, but physical disabilities, gender, economic background, and academic ability. The turmoil and trouble has brought us much closer to tolerance."

It warmed my heart when the students applauded. I wished that my husband Grant was alive to hear my speech. I had lunch with the school principal, several school board members, and a few students in the teachers' cafeteria. There was a nice write-up in the local paper. That was supposed to be the end of it, but it wasn't. At least not for me.

II Dresden

So, back to the tape recorder I went. This time it was for myself. Remembering . . .

I have lived in Dresden for thirty-plus years. It seems to me that I exited the civil rights struggle when my husband Grant and I moved here from the South. Dresden Union High School was asking me about my experiences in the outside world and not here. So I decided, all on my own, once my speech was over, to talk about this place, Dresden. Here, where I have lived, loved, and lost and more than likely will die.

If I am going to talk about Dresden, I need to talk about Grant first, even though it's hard for me to do. When Grant L. Harden, a seminary student from New England came to my small southern town, he was twenty-six and I was twenty-three. We fell in love amidst the turmoil of the civil rights struggle.

Grant was born in Westerbrook, Maine, the son of Virginie and Maxwell Harden and brother to Celeste and Sam. Grant's father was the headmaster of Sussex Fair Academy, a small private school in the town. His mother was the business manager and cook of the school. Grant described his mother as a tiny compact woman. She was efficient, hardworking, solemn, unemotional, and unapproachable. "Cold Fish," is how I described a woman I never met and whose son I loved. Virginie Harden died when Grant was sixteen. The next year Grant went to Dartmouth on a full scholarship. His brother and sister were not as academically gifted as he and got swallowed up by the early years of the drug culture. College and the seminary made Grant's split with his family complete.

When we met, Grant said that he felt as though he had no family.

I countered, "I have too much family. Loads of brothers and sisters and a Mama and Papa who are always messing in my business."

I didn't tell him that my family did a lot for me. I was feeling pretty cocky and sure of myself. I had won a scholarship to one of the finest black schools in the state and just graduated. I didn't acknowledge that I couldn't have done it without my uneducated parents' help and support. It took me a long time to tell Grant that and to admit it to myself.

Not Grant! I wanted to talk about Dresden .

Dresden is a college town, the home of Amberton College. Though I graduated from a black college, I never used my degree. Instead, I have a state license in cosmetology and do all kinds of hair. I'm not a skilled braider, so I have two African women who come up from Manchester, New Hampshire, once every two months to braid hair. There I go again, going off the point.

I have lived in Dresden for thirty-four years. I know its secrets and its stories. I know Amberton College, now University, as well, though strictly speaking I was never on the staff or a faculty member. Perhaps I'm a good one to talk about Dresden and Amberton because I'm an outsider. First, by the nature of my race and then by reason of my birth and upbringing. Finally, by virtue of my old age, in the world of youth and fast-moving change, Yet in the Dresden cemetery lies my husband and my son and sooner or later I will join them.

Before I started taping this again I went over to the historical society and the reading room at Amberton to find out the history of Dresden and the college. I can't get used to calling Amberton a university. That's too recent. Many people wonder which came first Amberton or the town of Dresden. Amberton is more well known than the town of Dresden. Historically speaking, the town known as Upper Dresden was incorporated in 1796 by a large extended family of Germans. Upper Dresden was a tiny hamlet surrounded by forest. Fifty-one years later, the first of the Amberton family came and built their English country manor on the hills above the town. Why did they come here, I wonder? I can't answer that. I know why Grant and I came here.

Grant went to Dartmouth, which is about 45 miles south of here. He'd come up to Amberton for dances and socializing because it was then a women's college and Dartmouth was an all-male school. But that is not why we settled here. When we came to Dresden, we were married and the world had fallen apart. In the space of several months two of the most important people in the world as we knew it had been murdered — Martin Luther King, Jr., and Robert F. Kennedy.

It seems to me (maybe not anyone else, but this is my opinion) that this was a time similar to the aftermath of 9/11. Shocked, grief stricken, and disillusioned, we looked for solace and safety in a place far away from the upheaval of the cities and the struggles of the South. We were the walking wounded when we came here. Grant was finishing his post-graduate work at the seminary and became the assistant to the chaplain at Amberton. More about that later.

Perhaps the remoteness is what attracted the Germans and then the Ambertons to Dresden, as it had us. The Amberton family made the bulk of their money on Wall Street. They married wealthy young New York socialites and retreated to Dresden to live in tranquil quiet. It would appear that the Amberton women were the ones who wanted to bring the culture and civilization of the city to their remote community. First, young ladies had extended visits to the Amberton estate and then came tutors, musicians, and artists to enrich their stay. A young ladies seminary grew out of this and then a college for women. What is notable in my mind is the fact that most of the inhabitants of Dresden are transplants like me. They've brought their unique backgrounds, culture, and characteristics with them. Dresden is the patchwork of all of us.

It amazes me when I think of comparing myself to the Amberton women. They were white socialites and debutantes when my ancestors were slaves. What brought Grant to the South and into my life was the social injustice of segregation. When we wanted to get married, we had to leave the South because marriage between people of different races was illegal in the state. An Episcopalian priest who had been one of Grant's professors married us in an Episcopal Church in New York City. It was my first trip to New York and we stayed there for nearly a year. Home in the South wasn't a safe place for either of us because of our civil rights work, and when we were married, it was even more dangerous. I would have been happy to stay in New York, but then the troubles began. First Martin Luther King, Jr., was assassinated and then Robert Kennedy. People seemed so angry, or maybe they were just hurt. I'm not sure.

I keep getting away from Dresden. Well, when I came here, Dresden was a small village with a small but well-known women's college. The town had the same number of inhabitants as the college had students. Dresden had a tiny elementary school (K–6) with fewer than a hundred students and Amberton College had its Lab School (Pre-K–3). The majority of the homeowners were employed by either the college or the Rebecca Amberton Memorial Clinic and Hospital, which is noted for its psychiatric/neurological wing. It is rumored that Elvis, the King, detoxed there. But I'm getting ahead of myself.

Dresden is a liberal enclave, one of a few in the state. To the south of us of course is Hanover, home of Dartmouth College. Maybe it was the liberal traditions that brought Grant and me here, and perhaps that is why I stayed after he died. Like I said before, Dresden is made up of exiles. People from as far off as South Africa and close by as the Northeast Kingdom of Vermont. Recently some Dartmouth professors moved to Dresden to avoid the high cost of property in Hanover. When I came here, it seemed that everyone I met was around my age and starting their professional and personal lives. Now it is quite the opposite. I am always the oldest person at any gathering.

There was little crime; no one locked their doors or their cars. Yet there was a coldness that was alien to my upbringing in the South. Northerners don't understand the complicated relationships between the races. When I was a teenager, my grandmother died. She had been a midwife and delivered many babies both black and white. People of every race from all around the county came to pay their respects to her. Whites stood outside the small country church, men with hats and caps in hand, women with starched and pressed dresses held handkerchiefs to their eyes. You knew your neighbors and their children. Years later when I went home to bury my mother, Miss Zina, a white woman in her eighties, came up to me in the local mini-mart and said, "You're Cora Mae, Ruby's girl, ain't you? Moved up North after you married that minister from up there."

And in the next breath, she added in a sincere voice, "I'm sorry for your loss. Your mama was a great God-fearing woman."

I had been gone for twenty years. In Dresden you could live next door to someone for twenty years and never enter their home and do no more than nod a greeting at them. You definitely didn't know anyone's background and if you did you kept it to yourself.

Maybe that wasn't a great example because certainly I had wonderful support when I lost Grant and my ten-year-old son Tomas, the fifth year of our stay in Dresden. Tomas, you may have gathered, wasn't Grant's child, but we won't talk about that now.

Grant got a small stipend in exchange for helping the Amberton College chaplain, Martin Baartmann, who was one of the descendants of the founding fathers of Dresden. Reverend Martin B. was one of the gentle and most peace-loving individuals I have ever known. Dr. Martin Luther King, Jr., had been a classmate of his at Crozier Theological Seminary, and Reverend Baartmann was consumed with grief at the loss of Dr. King.

One of Grant's duties was to run the Well-House, a community-outreach project sponsored by all the churches of Dresden. At the

Well-House they served coffee, had Bible study groups, and volunteer action committees that collected books and supplies for schools and churches in the South. Grant had informal counseling groups for troubled teenagers. Most of the volunteers at the Well-House were seniors (as I am now). They were women who baked muffins and kept the coffee urns filled. The name of the place referred to the enclosed communal wells mentioned in the Bible. People came to get water there, but they were also meeting places for the villagers. This modern-day wellhouse under Grant's leadership became the place for coffee and spiritual talk. Grant's slightly long dark hair that brushed against his clerical collar and steely blue-gray eyes presided over the place on most nights till closing times at ten-thirty.

I remember once a young guy was talking to Grant about the draft. He said, "I'm just one bad jump shot away from Vietnam."

"Or maybe Canada," Grant replied.

"Are you suggesting I go to Canada, Rev?" the young man challenged.

"No. I'm just saying that sometimes things that seem to have only one solution may have more than one."

It was an ideal place for Grant to expound his ideals and philosophy, as well as dispense his spiritual advice.

One night a woman came into the coffee house. I later learned that she was the wife of a young professor at the college. She sat down at a table.

"Can I help you?" I asked.

"I hear there's a priest . . . a guru who is better than any shrink. I've had my fill of shrinks." She was a pretty woman with long dark hair, slender, and with a wide full mouth. I always look at women's mouths. I have fat full lips; white people don't. Some of them seem to have no lips at all.

"What's your name?" I asked.

"Joyce Pantara."

"My husband isn't a priest," I explained. "But Grant likes to help people."

Grant walked over to us. He sat down with Joyce Pantara.

"I hate Dresden," she told him. "I hate my life."

"Why?"

"I'm not authentic. I have no face."

"What does that mean?"

"My husband is with the college. He is dying to get tenure. He thinks that's the ultimate."

"And you? What do you want?"

Not answering him, she continued, "Once I wanted a baby. Like my own trophy."

I watched them. It wasn't the first time that an attractive white woman had come on to Grant with that 'I'm helpless and lost' look in her eyes. Grant seemed somehow oblivious to their seductions. It wasn't until years later, when her book of short stories was published with its portrait of a thinly disguised Grant seduced by a beautiful, mentally distressed faculty wife, that I was able to feel justified in my suspicions. For a few months everyone seemed to be reading her book, and it was in the window of the bookstore. No one ever said anything to me about the similarities between the "priest" and Grant. In fact, most people didn't know him. Grant had been dead for years.

Was Grant faithful to me? I'm certain he was, but I was so insecure and uncertain back then that I fully expected him to leave me for someone prettier and, of course, white.

When we were alone in our bedroom, I always asked him, "Do you love me, Grant?"

"Of course, I do, Cora."

Sometimes, I cried.

"Why are you crying?" he had asked.

"Because I think someday you won't answer me that way."

It never happened. I don't know if it ever would have happened. As I wipe the tears from my eyes, I weep now that I didn't bask happily in that love while I had it.

It makes me remember Grant saying, "This I know. God is

love — unconditional love."

I listened like the others, but there was something in me that made it impossible to believe what he was saying. I had been brought up believing that we were unworthy and had to be punished for our wickedness. I know I had plenty to be punished for.

While he was in Boston at the seminary defending his thesis, Grant wrote me a letter (one of the few I received from him and kept).

Dear Cora,

We haven't talked about our major difference. I hope you know it isn't race. It is, of course, religion. It has been a long solitary journey for me — my father subscribed to the proprieties of being a headmaster of a formerly religious school. Going to church was part of the protocol and nothing more.

I had a divine revelation when I was a freshman at Dartmouth. I didn't reveal my embracing Christ to my family until I won a fellowship to the theological seminary.

Finding you has made me see that this journey to Christ need not be lonely. In a spiritual reading book I received from a Catholic friend a prayer began, "Come let us ascend together with the Holy Spirit."

My Darling, I offer you my hand, my heart, my life .
Grant

And I tried to ascend with him. In my youth, I sang in the choir, I listened to long sermons about the fires of hell and damnation, and watched the sisters down home getting the spirit. For me religion was part of a ritual and a routine. For Grant it was something more. He truly had faith. And as long as I had him, I had it too. Even now, I believe that Grant and Tomas are in Heaven. But I'm not sure if I'll ever see them again. I'm not a churchgoer or a religious person, but I do believe in God. How else could I have met and married such a man as Grant?

III A Life in Dresden

Opening a hair salon was the furthest thing from my mind when Grant and I moved here. I was certified to teach elementary school back home and thought I would be able to teach here once we were settled. I discovered much to my dismay that there wasn't reciprocity with my home state. My credentials were not acceptable. I worked for a time as an educational assistant at the Amberton Lab School. I could have, had we been able to afford it, taken the necessary education courses needed to qualify to teach. But we couldn't afford it. Reverend Martin Baartmann's health was failing and we wondered if Grant might take his place. That was not to be. Grant, also, talked about returning to the South, even though the political climate had changed there. It was the rise of the Black Panthers and the Black Muslims — separation on our own terms was the cry of the new black leaders. Integration had failed and died with Martin Luther King, Jr., they said.

I made a life for myself in Dresden. At first I worked (had a chair) in someone else's salon. That job happened by chance. It was several months after Grant died. I still volunteered in the Well-House. That's where I met Maurice and Jolie, French Canadians, who owned their own shop in Dresden. They offered me a job helping out in their beauty shop.

What a time of change for me! I had to learn how to drive — I was against it, of course. After all a car accident had killed Grant and Tomas and injured me. But I needed to drive if I was to continue to live in Dresden, and I was determined to stay as far away from my family as possible. I needed something more than my part-time work as a teacher aide at the Amberton Lab School. Our rent-free apartment above the Well-House was mine until the end of the year or longer if the replacement for Grant didn't need housing.

"Corie," Maurice said to me one afternoon after I had been working there several months, "I want to ask you something. Have you ever had your hair straightened by chemicals?"

"Yes," I replied. I thought of how Grant had disapproved of straighteners. He told me my hair was beautiful in its natural state, and out of respect for him, I wore it unstraightened. I tied my unruly kinky hair up with scarves. Now that Grant was gone, I could wear my hair any way I wanted to.

"It is necessaire," Maurice explained to me, "to be able to do all kinds of processes on hair to get licensed in the States. In Montreal we have many black people, but here there are only a few. Jolie must do the exam for her license. You want to get license like Jolie?"

"Yes, I want to get my license," I answered.

"Will you come home with us to Montreal where we will do a, how you say, clinique? Then you and Jolie can get your licenses."

It was my first trip out of the States. Maurice cut and styled my hair after Jolie straightened it. While I was training with Maurice, I did shampoos and some simple treatments. I took occasional trips to Montreal to work on West Indian and Haitian people who lived there. I believe that Jolie hoped that I would find a new mate among the transplanted exiles from the French and British Caribbean islands. In a way, I loved the foreign feeling of the West Indian neighborhoods of Montreal. I liked the food, the smells, but I always felt ill at ease and longed to return to Dresden where I understood the nuances and rhythms of the people so much better.

The beauty shop came later. It is on the side street off the main thoroughfare of Dresden. Over the years, it has become a fixture. I have never had to advertise in the over twenty-five years of its existence. Young African-American coeds seem to find me. They come with all kinds of preconceived notions about what I know about hair care for black women. They also come with their individual stories of how they came to Dresden and Amberton. Some don't want to have their hair done at all, they just want to talk with an older African-American woman. They miss their mamas and aunties. I get African-American college professors as well. Some even come up from Dartmouth, though many of them prefer to travel to Boston to the sophisticated and pricey salons there. My clients are not only African-Americans. Some of my oldest are the long-time white residents of Dresden and environs.

IV Family

Another thing that got me thinking about recording these memories is that Buddy Jr., my nephew, called last night. What seemed strange to me was that he was on his cell phone in his truck and his wife Janet was in the house having a meeting of the African-American Heritage Club. His excuse was that he needed to use up his extra minutes for the month.

Buddy Jr. is the closest to me of all my nieces and nephews, perhaps it has to do with the fact that his father Buddy was the closest of all my brothers and sisters. A few years ago my brother Buddy passed away. I hate that terminology. Why did I use it? I swore to myself that I would never use it like all the church women of my past did. Buddy died of prostrate cancer, heart disease, or maybe just a broken heart. I am the only one left of Ulysses Marquette and Ruby Marquette's ten children. I have loads of nieces and nephews, grandnieces and nephews and a few great grand ones, as well. Buddy Jr. and his wife don't have children after twelve years of marriage. Janet is a teacher at Gordonsville Elementary School.

Buddy Jr. said, "Aunt Cora, I know you're pretty independent, just like Daddy was, but I just want you to think about the fact that you're the last one left. All this land, nearly a hundred acres, belongs to you. And you don't have any children. Anything happens to you, without any provisions, we might lose the land after all your papa and mama did to get it for us."

I didn't speak, but inside I wondered if he was calling me and being kind to me so that I'd leave the land to him.

"You ever think of coming back home?" he said. His voice seemed guileless, and I felt ashamed for harboring such thoughts about him. Still, did I really know him? Does he know me?

Perhaps the only way to explain how I feel is to go back to that awful time, after Grant and Tomas died. My family never understood my feelings for Grant. They thought they understood him. They thought he was a naive white boy who was playing at integration. They thought I was a rebellious young woman who thought she was better than them. When Grant died, there was no sympathy from anyone in my family. My mother was still smarting from my taking Tomas away from her. She had raised him from birth, giving me the opportunity to accept a college scholarship, and I had taken him away without so much as a by-your-leave. I had always had a difficult relationship with my mother. She was worn out from hard work and childbearing when I was born. She gave Tomas, her grandchild, all the love I felt she had denied me. I claimed my son with a hurt and proud arrogance that I regret now all these years later. I guess the greatest blow was the fact that I buried Tomas up here alongside Grant. There is a place for me next to the two of them. Buddy, my brother, came up to the funeral, to represent the family, I guess.

"Cora, you hurt Mama to her heart," he said then. "You know she loved your boy more than life."

"I know she loved him, but he was my boy. My son. We were accepted here as a family, and that's where they should be laid to rest."

I was so sure of myself. My grief and my pain added to my self-righteousness. It was a final rift between my family and me, with the exception of Buddy. My father was dead, and years later my mother died too. My brothers and sisters and their families became distant strangers.

V My Life in Dresden

One day an Amberton coed came rushing into Maurice's shop without an appointment. She was strikingly beautiful in a well-scrubbed Scandinavian blonde sort of way.

"I need some style, something new and altogether different," she demanded as she held up her long wavy blonde hair.

"N'est pas possible," Maurice said in French.

"Pourquoi non?" she answered him. Jolie was away and Maurice and I were the only ones in the shop.

"I am completely booked. You must have an appointment," he said.

She glanced my way and appraised me with her large expressive blue eyes.

"Would you do my hair?" she asked.

Maurice interrupted, "Corie, do you have an appointment?" he knew I didn't. Something made me decide not to play games with the young woman.

With Maurice looking on watchfully, I trimmed a few inches off her hair and styled it. She smiled at the way her hair looked when I handed her a mirror. It was my first serious hair styling.

"This is the beginning of a beautiful friendship," she said. "I'm Meredith,' she said as she extended her hand.

"And I'm Cora, though Maurice insists on calling me Corie."

"I like Corie better," she answered.

Later I discovered she was a sophomore at Amberton. She became my regular customer. Two things stood out about Meredith. The first was that she seemed totally oblivious to how beautiful she was. She never seemed to notice how people stared at her with gaping mouths and surprised faces. Even Maurice, who was old enough to be her father and devoted to his Jolie, was smitten by Meredith. That truly impressed me. I admired Meredith for insouciance in the face of the admiration for her incredible beauty.

The second thing had to do with me — she never commented, or seemed in any way aware of the fact that I was black and she was white and that it was somehow unusual or even noteworthy that I did her hair. When I moved to my own shop, she followed me. Often when the shop was full of black women, Meredith sat and waited her turn. She watched as I put chemical relaxers on kinky hair and occasionally, in the old days, straightened hair with a hot comb. She was fascinated with the African braiders who came to work at my shop. Don't get me wrong, Meredith wasn't silent.

"Is that harmful to your hair?" she asked my customers, not me. Meredith laughed and said, "Of course, Corie's not going to say it is. Is it expensive? I don't think I could sit still long enough to get my hair braided."

Some of the young black women were taken aback by Meredith and mistrustful. Others ignored her. After she graduated, Meredith left Dresden for a few years, but she returned and opened a private investigation agency. Over the years she became that rare thing — a true and honest friend.

I have always made a point to be especially cordial whenever I see a new black person in town. I know what it means to be a stranger among a sea of white faces. I did that with Sarah Clarke when she became a professor of Black Studies at the college. Her reaction was to smile timidly at me. She seemed too shy and reserved to respond any more than that. When she came to Amberton, she was an overweight black woman with thin processed short hair. I asked students who were my customers about her. They told me she was brilliant, but her baggy pants suits and lack of style made her in their eyes either an object of pity or scorn. It took a major illness that caused her to lose over seventy pounds and all her hair to transform her into the attractive stylish woman she is now.

I remember the day she came to me, her head covered with a big woolen cap.

"My hair, what little I have is coming out," she said in a weak tremulous voice.

"Let me see I said." Gently, I pulled the cap off her head. There were bald spots in several places.

Her large brown eyes filled with tears. "All my life people have laughed at me —singing Fatty, fatty two by four. They made fun of my big lips and pimply dark skin. I can't bear it. Sometimes I think I'll stop the radiation and chemo and just die."

"Don't talk like that," I said to her. "Your life is precious. You're a brilliant woman and a fine teacher."

I called Maurice and Jolie, who had moved back to Montreal by then. I could hardly understand Maurice any longer. I was sure that Jolie, whose English had always been shaky at best, must now speak only French. Without hesitation, Maurice agreed to come down to Dresden to help with Sarah Clarke's problem. He brought five different real hair wigs for Professor Clarke to try on.

"À bien," he said in his combination of French and English. She doesn't know me. You have her trust. It is best to shave her head. You try the wigs on her. Alone without other people. Let her have her dignity. Et moi, she never sees me. You are her friend. Only you can see, n'est pas? You comprehend?"

"Yes," I said. By then I knew something about life and felt with her the fear and pain of living. For a short time her anguish became mine. I know that after that Sarah Clarke mattered to me and I think I mattered to her too.

I ask myself, did Dr. Darise Wyatt and her daughter Xanda come to Dresden before Professor Sarah Clarke or after? Now, Xanda Wyatt may be more beautiful than Meredith Northern, or maybe it is just my prejudice. Xanda Wyatt made me wonder if Grant and I had had a daughter if she would have looked like Xanda. There were traces of Dr. Darise, her mother, in Xanda. She had large expressive eyes and the same large sensuous mouth as her mother. Her eyes were hazel, green though and not brown like her mother's. Xanda's skin was creamy beige and she had soft silky brown hair with natural blonde highlights. Unlike Meredith, even as a very young child, Xanda Wyatt was aware of her great beauty. There was something about her that exuded an air of superiority, especially toward the African-American patrons of my shop. Xanda was not as kind or compassionate as her mother. Once when she noticed that other African-American women had extensions braided into their hair, a pre-teenage Xanda wondered out loud if that made the braids less authentic. The African women answered her that hair was just hair and not true beauty. I hoped that they had taught her a lesson.

On the other hand, Dr. Darise continually apologized for what she believed were Xanda's insensitive remarks. A child psychologist, Dr. Darise seemed to understand every child but her own. This made me sad and wonder if children were often the cause of as much pain as joy.

"Cora, do you feel at home here in Dresden?" Dr. Darise Wyatt asked me.

"Yes, I'm at peace here. There are no surprises and all the dramas are behind closed doors and secret."

"Well, it's different than the South, I hear.

"Dresden is unique, in my mind," I said.

"You're right about that," Darise replied with a bitterness in her voice. Her eyes blazed and there was a slight tremor in her hands. I was amazed at her outburst.

"Dresden is a small duchy of intellectual aristocratic parvenus mixed with pseudo rural folks. They pride themselves on their cultural artifacts such as the summer stock playhouse, the small writers and artistic colony, and of course, the college. They adhere to a strict code of secrecy, no matter the cost. Even death."

Darise paused a moment, and I put her under the dryer. It stopped the talk for about fifteen minutes. I gazed out the window at the Dresden street, trying to ease my own nervous reaction to her words. Window boxes of late spring flowers crowded the shops and bank windows. In all the years she had lived in this town, I had never seen Dr. Darise stroll down the street. When I see her, she is walking with a purpose — going somewhere urgently. Grant and I strolled down the street together. Now I walk alone, but I walk with him in my heart. Somehow I feel walking brings you closer to a place than driving around and through it.

When Darise emerged from the dryer, she was in a very different mood. I was glad of that. I thought I understood why she had spoken out so bitterly. Her only child was leaving to go off to college in New York City, and she was devastated. She had invested her entire life in Xanda. Somehow Dr. Darise weathered the years without her daughter and continued to work as a child psychologist in Dresden. When Xanda graduated from college, she stayed in New York City and Darise stayed in Dresden alone.

That was the only outburst I ever witnessed from Dr. Darise. I felt her sadness and tried to be a friend without overstepping the boundaries she set. I always felt that Dr. Darise never fully revealed herself to me or anyone else, but then I believe you shouldn't have to know a person's secrets in order to love and care about them.

In fact, I think learning someone's secrets doesn't tell you very much about the person. All you learn are their secrets. You still don't know who they are. That takes looking into their hearts and listening to them talk about ordinary things without judgment or ridicule.

I never married after Grant, but in my own way I gave my heart again. Certainly not in the same way that I had given it to Grant. For a number of years there was Walter, a Polish man, a cabinetmaker, who lived across the river from Dresden. During the nineties Walter had a major carpentry project at the college — a restoration. Walter and I first met as regulars at the Dresden Coffee Shop in the Cinema building. The Dresden Coffee Shop is run by Stella LaPlante. Her brother Serge is the cook. I'd stop there every morning for breakfast. I'd have the country breakfast and a medium-sized coffee. That would last me for the entire day. I never required much food and what I eat, I burn up. My weight hasn't fluctuated more than ten pounds in the last twenty years.

Walter is a big man, balding. I was shocked to discover he was nearly ten years my junior. I liked to cook for Walter. He made me laugh with his crazy mixed-up accented English. My stories of the South were like stories of a foreign country to him. His stories of Poland had one common theme, his real life was there. They were his real people. We shared our different backgrounds with each other and in a way our foreignness bound us together.

"More than anything else in the world, I want to be a father," he told me. It was one of our early dates. The dates followed a pattern. He came to my house, we had dinner, watched television or a video, and sometimes he stayed over. That was usually on a Friday night, never on Saturdays. He had church on Sundays.

"Children are God's gift," I told him often. It was something Grant always said. When Grant and I got married, I felt guilty because I couldn't get pregnant with his child. I was convinced that Grant wanted his own child and that Tomas would never be enough for him. Grant said, "Children are God's gift whether they are from your body or not."

Walter didn't feel that way. Even before I told him I wasn't able to have children, I knew he didn't want to have children with me. My vanity made me not tell him that I was too old. It didn't matter.

For the year 2000 Walter made plans to go to Poland to celebrate with his elderly mother and sister who was a former nun. He talked continuously about the trip for the millennium celebration. He marveled that he and the Pope would celebrate in their mother country on such a momentous occasion.

Quickly I tired of hearing about his trip when I realized that I would have no part in this celebration. Not once did he ask me if I would like to go to Poland with him. I who had been his girlfriend for seven years. Perhaps girlfriend is the wrong term, but I can't bring myself to use any other word and perhaps there is none to describe what I was to him.

Unlike Walter, Grant took me to the banquet table with him. Walter was more like Tomas's father, an itinerant fruit picker who was also an artist. Ernesto (Tomas's father) had skirted the announcement that he had a black girlfriend for fear of being ostracized by his fellow Mexican farm workers. Guilelessly honest, he answered when I asked him if he would have told his fellow workers if I had been white. He smiled and answered, "Si. My friends would respect me for making an Anglo love me."

It was too late then. I was sixteen and already pregnant with Tomas.

"For the new millennium," I said to Walter, " I'm starting a new page. I'm cutting away all the deadwood. I'm severing ties with those who don't respect me and care about me."

"I care about you," he added too quickly.

"No, you don't, Walter. You've never taken me to church with you. You never once asked me to meet any members of the Polish community. And your big trip — you've never included me."

"It's very expensive," he tried to explain.

"When you come back from Poland, it will be a new century. I take that seriously. In the last century, my people, though free from slavery had to fight a terrible oppression. We couldn't ride buses and sit where we wanted, we could not attend schools that we wanted to, we had to live in a world where, from the cradle to the grave, we were treated as inferior. One by one, after hard-earned fights, the laws changed, but often people's hearts didn't.

"I am here in Dresden, a resident of Dresden because my late husband thought we would be safe here and our children could live and flourish here. So, I will not begin a new century observing the old rules and traditions. I will not hide or sneak around with you, Walter."

He was hurt. He called after he returned. He sent me a New Year's card from Krakow. I didn't budge. A year later I saw his picture in the paper with his new bride a woman in her forties from Poland with three teenage children.

Both Dr. Darise and Professor Sarah agreed that what I did was wise.

"You should have told me you were alone on New Year's Eve. A friend of mine — a doctor, came up from New York City and we toasted in 2000," Sarah said.

Dr. Darise added, trying not to sound like a psychologist, but not succeeding, "How do you feel about breaking off with him?"

"I feel great," I said. I made a fake smile and held it for a few moments. Both Sarah and Darise were sitting under dryers that had just clicked off.

"Xanda will be up from New York on the five-thirty," Darise informed us. "She has something to tell me, I think it may be she's seeing someone seriously."

Sarah Clark and I looked at each other and smiled. Xanda had made that announcement several times. Each time when the romance had faded, Darise seemed to be more devastated than her daughter. Gradually the pain of breaking up with Walter lessened. Through the years they supported me and I supported them. In some ways I still miss Walter, but I am happy that I haven't settled. I wish him well.

Then there was my family. My brother Buddy tried to reconcile me with with my oldest sister Noreen. He brought her up for a visit. She sniffed around my house, trying to find fault. She did give me a grudging compliment on my garden, too many flowers but the tomatoes were good. Buddy drove her around showing her that the mountains and trees were reminiscent of home.

But she just wondered how I could live with so many white people. Wondered if I missed being with my own. Times changed for her as well. Her favorite son married a white girl and moved to Atlanta. Noreen died years ago long, before I lost Buddy. Noreen's favorite son, my nephew, is married to a black woman now (so Buddy Jr. tells me), and she is raising his two children by his first wife, as well as their three sons. I don't know any of their names.

And so it goes, Buddy Jr. asked me again if I wanted to retire down home. I hesitated. For a moment I thought of the church cemetery down there that holds all my siblings, my parents, and all my other relatives for generations, as well as those who gave their lives in the civil rights struggle. But then Dresden holds me too. My roots go deep here. There are people I care about here. There is Professor Sarah, Dr. Darise, Meredith, and many more. Unlike my sister Noreen's children, I know their names and then too the Dresden cemetery holds a piece of my heart and a place for me as well.

I have to stop now. Professor Sarah will be here soon. She is dragging me into the twenty-first century. Amberton is revamping its computer system, and Sarah has gotten a used computer for me. She says I'm going to be hooked up to the Internet and will be able to send and receive e-mails.

"How will I do that?"

"I have signed you up for a computer class at the Well-House Senior Center," she told me. "Yes, you can do this, Cora. You have to do this, because I will be at Capetown University for the next two semesters and you have to talk to me."

When I told Meredith, she said she wanted to be in on it too. She'll be here soon. I made my cinnamon coffee cake and a pot of decaf. Meredith also said that now that I'm a celebrity at Dresden Union High School since my speech, I probably can get a personal tech adviser from the school. I really have to stop talking and get ready for my friends who make my life worth living here in Dresden.

Joyce's Tale: A Novella

I A Necessary Death

We had only been in Dresden for a few weeks when the daughter of the president of Amberton College died. My husband Stephen, a new faculty member, and I attended the memorial service that was held in the college chapel. An older faculty member told us that it was an exception to hold Amelia Rose's service in the college chapel since she was neither a student, faculty member, nor an alumna. As newcomers, Stephen and I did not know or appreciate the significance of this break with precedent and tradition. We didn't know that this indicated a crack or rent in the delicate fabric of things.

Stephen had been hired as an assistant professor in the English department on the tenure track. The college represented it as a step up in the echelons of academia, while being a severe pay cut from the community and technical colleges of the outer boroughs of New York City where he had labored for the last five years.

Dresden, a tiny village nestled in a valley between the Green and the White Mountains, has the college as its center. Forty-five minutes from Dartmouth College with its libraries and art and cultural center; the college held a unique fascination for Stephen. He was a stranger to small-town life, having grown up in the Bronx. We came to Dresden because I was pregnant, and we thought this would be an ideal place for us to raise a family and further his career. Unfortunately, I miscarried before we left New York City. It left me at loose ends. I had no direction and perhaps that accounts for what happened later.

The miscarriage came as we were preparing to leave New York

and move to Dresden. Stephen was bringing to a close his tenure at Long Island Tech and putting the finishing touches on his thesis at Columbia. I had quit my job at the Schomburg Library in Harlem. Though Stephen's sister offered to come over and help when I had the miscarriage, I told her it was all right. I packed up the baby clothes, toys, and blankets we had received from well-wishers and sent them ahead with our other things to Dresden.

By the time we got to Dresden, I was beginning to believe that we had handled the loss well and plunged enthusiastically into making our faculty housing into a home. There was no plan for what I would do while Stephen pursued his teaching duties.

The faculty and students seated in the college chapel overpowered me. I recognized only a few of the people. I was still trying to put names with faces. There had been a round of "get acquainted" cocktail parties. Everyone was a blur except a few people. There was Bill Harrison, the head of the English department and his wife Norma. I found her a strikingly attractive and sophisticated woman — like the kind you would meet in New York City if you were invited to the right parties, though Stephen and I didn't travel in those circles. L. I. Tech didn't have cocktail parties. Despite that, it was that New York City I missed and longed for.

Norma Harrison seemed to shine above the other wives even at the memorial service for the president's daughter. Norma wore a smart sleeveless black sheath that came to a little above her knees and showed off her long shapely legs. A single strand of pearls hung around her neck, her short dark hair was pushed behind her ears to reveal one pair of pearl stud earrings and in addition a pair of diamond studs. The fact that her ears were pierced twice made a statement about her. It made me hope that she would be my friend.

I recognized a black couple. I didn't remember their names, but I thought he was in the history department, and his wife was a child psychologist. They had a little girl—a toddler.

"Amelia Rose Parker," the college chaplain intoned, "though not a student, was the same age as the freshman class. Had her life been different she would be with them exploring the wonders of literature, science, and philosophy. Instead, she graced the halls and walkways of the college with her warm affectionate and beautiful innocence. Her radiance, her delight in the simple joys of nature make her brief time here with us precious for all who knew her."

Even in my brief time here, I had seen the slight girl with the curly blonde hair and large vacant blue eyes. I was struck by her tiny feet and hands, her slender frame that looked as though a strong wind could knock her over. She was never alone. Either one of her parents or another adult supervised and guided her. Students and others made way for her, keeping their distance. In some ways, I felt akin to her. I, too, walked the campus but was not a part of the college. The next person to speak was Norma Harrison. "Goodbye, sweet Amelia Rose. Farewell to your smile, your affectionate hugs. I could dwell on all we've lost, but that is too painful, instead I want to celebrate what you gave to us. Some people may say that a handicapped person can't give to those who aren't. Those people saw Amelia as a burden and responsibility. Anyone who says that about her didn't know sweet Amelia Rose. She was joy, purity, and innocence. She was a gift to her parents Arthur and Roberta and to all of us."

Norma returned to her seat. Stephen whispered, "Norma Harrison is a published poet."

President Parker thanked everyone for coming, and then it was over. We left the chapel and headed to the banquet hall. Outside the chapel the brilliant colors of fall overwhelmed me. Stephen and I walked silently through the multicolored leaves. He was off in his thoughts and I in mine. I stopped myself from asking him what he was thinking. I had learned in the seven years we had been together that it was better not to ask. I thought of my own deaths — my father when I was ten and my unborn child.

I discovered Stephen wasn't thinking about our unborn child's death when I overheard his conversation with another junior faculty member. Rick Riccibono, who was a second-year faculty member, huddled with Stephen. They had plates of food balanced precariously on their knees. They were like two teenage boys watching the grown-ups. I headed toward them, wanting to take my place by my husband's side until I heard their conversation.

Rick Riccibono was in the language department. He was recently divorced. He had split with his young wife during his first year at the college. In contrast to Stephen's dark good looks, Rick was a big athletic man with sandy hair and a plain face.

Rick said, "Well, I think they handled that very well or as well as one could under the circumstances. Little Amelia Rose certainly made her presence known. She was a drooling, stumbling nuisance in adult-sized diapers, and I bet secretly Mr. and Mrs. Prez are breathing a sigh of relief that she has been plucked from this mortal coil."

Stephen replied, "So, you think that despite their protestations to the contrary, the Parkers are relieved that their daughter is gone? Her death, in fact, is their ticket out of here and on to a bigger and better venue."

Rick smirked. "You're catching on, my friend. Mark my word, Stephen, Parker's on the fast track now that the little embarrassing bundle of joy is out of the way."

I put my plate down and moved away from my husband, not waiting to hear anything else he or Rick had to say. I wanted Stephen to defend the Parkers, to protest that people were not liars and hypocrites. Had I landed in a place where polite facades were just a cover for lies, deceit, and treachery? I wasn't sure. What I was sure of was that I was on my own, I was alone in a strange place, without a friend or a job, and childless.

II Joyce's Journals

Now in my journal I write:

I thought today when I walked back to the house from town that I would like to stay here in Dresden until I'm very old. I didn't always feel that way. At first I missed New York, but I've gotten used to it here. The sky is a winter gray. Someone says that means it's going to snow. It's the kind of morning, I imagine, one could be depressed about; but I am not. I like the walk into town. I like the solitary sound of the dead leaves crunching under my feet. I came to Dresden over a year ago with my husband Stephen. It has been hard to adjust. This past summer I had another miscarriage. Stephen got me into therapy and thinks that will make it all right. I don't have a job or a purpose. My only outlet is to write in this journal. Is that enough to keep me going?

Stephen is coming out of the shower. I'll write later.

"Steve, coffee?"

"Yes, honey."

"The New York Times isn't in yet. I'll go back around ten. What time's your class?"

"No classes today. I'm going to work in my office until the faculty meeting at one-thirty."

Stephen is standing in the doorway to the bedroom, a towel around his neck and nothing else on. Smile. Take my picture with a Polaroid. Is this what they mean by open marriage?

"What did they call the other way that people made coffee?" I ask my husband.

"Percolate," he answers. "Why?"

"Just wondered. I couldn't remember what they called it."

"What are you doing today?" Stephen asks uncharacteristically. "Why?"

"Just asking," he says. He eyes me uncomfortably.

"I see Dr. Sumner today. I see Dr. Sumner three times a week, Stephen, you know that."

Maybe Stephen will ask me to take a drive around the lake. He doesn't.

I ask him, "Maybe after the doctor's we could take a drive around the lake."

"Joyce, I don't have time for such nonsense. I have a faculty meeting and then I've got to go back to the office to work."

"On your article on the transcendental poets?"

"Yes. Why?"

"I just wondered. I thought I'd write today myself." I try to sound casual.

"Do you think you should? Have you discussed this with Dr. Sumner? Why don't you look for my brown corduroy jacket and take it to the cleaners. Then it'll be time to go to the doctor.

Stephen, as usual, leaves me alone for the day.

Now I write in my journal:

It has been a long time since I wrote that. Weeks. Months. I don't remember. Even though the snow is deep, I walked into town to get the paper. I got the New York Times as usual. I didn't buy the Boston Globe. I don't know Boston. I used to live in New York. My boots make deep footprints in the fresh snow. Once I made a snowball and brought it into the house and put it on Stephen's empty plate. It melted and all that he saw was a plate of dirty water. He didn't say anything. It was in his eyes. Joyce is crazy. When is she going to get better? Now I write poetry. At least I think it's poetry.

Inside the house. In a corner. Under the bed. Knife in the pocket. Knife at the throat. Danger. Dangerous.

No one has seen this. Maybe I'll show it to Norma Harrison. She writes poetry. No, not yet. Maybe later.

Now in my journal I write:

Spring is the mischief in me. Spring will be a little late this year.

April is the cruelest month. April in Paris . . . Will I live to see April? Do I want to? Dr. Sumner says I shouldn't write this. I showed him something, and he said he didn't understand where it came from.

Bloodon the poem shit onthe typing paper motherofgod sixhundredpills of alldescription thankyoufor thinkingof ourmagazinebut yourworkdoesn't meet our needsatthe present congratulations it's a dead babyboy.

Morgan is Dr. Sumner's first name. Was it wise to air one's dirty laundry in Dresden? Too late. I already did.

Now in my journal I write:
Stephen and I were invited to the head of the department's house for drinks and conversation last night. Amazingly enough, someone wanted my opinion about something. Norma Harrison was working on a poem and asked me to listen to it. She gave me a copy. I'm including it.

Birthday Dinner

The October
Betty Crocker Cookbook Calendar
featured
smothered stuffed pork chops

For his October birthday,
She made the chops
Bedecked the table with flowers
to look the same
Perfection

He sent the skillet sailing across the floor
Grease, tomatoes, peppers, meat

defacing polished tiles
This his only thank you
to her Technicolor picture
of their life.

"I always thought poetry had to be pretty," I said.
"Life isn't always pretty," Norma answered. "Poetry is life. Life is poetry."

Now in my journal I write:
Stephen destroyed the evening for me.
"You can't criticize her poetry, Joyce. Her husband is my boss. Find yourself someone else to hang out with."
"But wouldn't it be better for me to cultivate Norma Harrison in furtherance of your tenure plot?" I said, trying to sound flip and not desperate. "Maybe if I spend time with her . . ."
"Joycie," Stephen interrupted, "You don't know how things work."
"Of course, I don't know how anything works. I don't know anything. I don't even know myself."
I was surprised when Norma called me, but I was obedient and put her off until she didn't call anymore. All I got from her was the desire to write poetry of my own.
Stephen thinks because he's a college professor he knows everything, not just about his field, but about the world. It reminds me that they called my father the professor. It was not a compliment but an accusation that he thought he was better than the other teachers at Palmer High School. He was a serious scholar or so he wanted everyone to believe; instead he just wanted to stay away from his wife and gaze at the pictures of the bronze statues of the Greek gods he loved. My mother used the term "professor" as a sign of endearment. She adored him.
Stephen is the same as my father. But I'm not my mother.
Now I write in Joyce's Journal:

Then the knife hit the skin tore into it liketeeth and bloodspit out onto the clean whitesheet. I'm sorry but we can't stop usingyou. Come onbaby shakethat thing. My name is James. What's yours? Joyciejoyciejoyciejoycie. That's the Harvard Library. No I went to BU, my sister went to Radcliffe. Firsttime in boston, honey. you aint seennothin'tillyou'vebeen in a motelbaby like theholidayinn. the smell of frenchcigarettesand poetry. I write poetry too. will i have manyloversbesidehim. sixteen thattime take sixteen everyfourhours. nodoctorsaid that. It's your fault your babies died. what's wrong with you baby? are you on something, honey? i gotta call Morgan. who's morgan? your husband? your doctor? i'm out of here, baby.

Journal entry:
Must not call Morgan. Must stop referring to the shrink by his first name. Isn't that too familiar? Morgan is here? Married? Not married. Did you come? What's that scar? You have children? Stillborn. I'll call you tomorrow. Burn it. Burn them all. I stand before you naked lost unloved love me. Rising out of the crowd in slow motion a lone black face coming toward the stage. Gimmeshelter mickjaggerhelp. Stephen, I'm in Boston. I should have gone home to New York. I had to get away. I'll be back tomorrow. Click.

Now in my journal I write:
I'll remember April and be sad. glad?
The receptionist at the clinic seems surprised to see me. I am certain that I have an appointment with Morgan. I wish I could remember his last name. It really doesn't matter.
The receptionist comes back to me and says that Dr. Sumner will see me. Dr. Sumner — that's his name.
"Hello, Morgan," I say.
"How are you, Joyce?"
"FINE. I FIND THE WEATHER INVIGORATING, DON'T YOU?"
"Joyce, you are standing next to me, you needn't talk so loud.

Are you all right?"

"I'M FINE AND YOU?"

"Joyce, do you know that you don't have an appointment with me? Do you know what the date is, Joyce?"

"April is the cruelest month . . . Are we just April fools," I sing a little. "I'm so glad to see you, Morgan." I can't call him Dr. Sumner, it's too formal. We are intimates.

"Joyce, what are you writing?"

"You know, it's my journal, Doctor . . . Morgan. Remember? I told you about it in Boston."

"Boston?"

"Remember Boston, Morgan?"

"Joyce, are you taking any medication?

"YES, THANK YOU. IT'S A LOVELY DAY ISN'T IT, MORGAN?"

"Joyce, I'm going to have to call your husband. You'll need to be sedated and hospitalized.

His mouth was cruel and the kiss bruised my soul.

III Letters to and from Dresden

Journal entry:

I have been banished from Dresden for my sins. So, I'm copying the letters I received and sent or meant to send into my journal. I can't bring myself to read the other things I wrote. My journals are too full of mad gibberish. That was the crime that has me exiled here in the South with my elderly mother. I was mad in Dresden and that is not acceptable, especially not for Stephen.

Maybe I should explain Dresden. Dresden is a tiny New England town on the cusp of the divide between New Hampshire and Vermont. Here a wealthy family founded a female seminary, which developed into a women's college. The college is the center of the town. The townspeople are a mixture of locals and the people who earned their living through the college. Stephen, my husband, and I came to Dresden after he had spent five years teaching English at Long Island Tech College while I worked as a children's librarian at the Schomburg branch of the New York Public Library in Harlem.

In a little less than two years, I have had two miscarriages. It is unlikely that I shall ever have any children. I have very few friends in Dresden. Come to think of it, I have very few friends anywhere. Still, I did get letters and did attempt to write some.

Dear Joyce,

Dresden is as always. Ice. Ice in your drinks. On the roads. Ice in people's hearts. Anne and Jack Macklin's marriage (You remember them, don't you? He teaches Romantic Poetry) is very shaky. I've never seen it to fail, he gets tenure, they buy the house, the children are doing well in school, and then things fall apart. It seems success does that to people these days. I'm not sure who's involved in their breakup. It would be refreshing if no one was. People's relationships here are positively incestuous.

How are you? I've seen your husband Stephen around, but he

just grunts at me. From the look of him, he really needs you back. Maybe just in time for mud season. There's been little snow this winter and skiing was nonexistent, not that I give a damn. It's just been an incredibly cold gray winter.

The good news is that The Press is publishing my new book. I'll send you a copy. There are some poems you heard last fall at the reading before you got sick.

How's Virginia? Do you know, I have never been to Virginia except to Williamsburg. Bill did a paper on colonial American writers (his specialty, in case you forgot), and the people there wanted him to consult on a new exhibit that never materialized. I was bored out of my mind for nearly a week. We did stop in Washington and I saw a new Miller play at the Kennedy Center.

Tell me, are you all rested up and can you come back soon? I miss your fresh perspective on poetry. In the summer I'm going to give another reading. If you have anything, perhaps you could read too. Take care and be glad you've had a winter sabbatical from Dresden.

Norma

P.S. Here's a poem I've been working on. What do you think?

Cookie Cutter Life

Girl shape
Bow mouth
Shiny hair
Trim figure
Too crisp
Too brittle
Old age creeps in
a foreign shape
The mold cracks
The face shifts
The breasts sag
Life's too short

Dear Norma,

Your letter was such a joy. Everyone who writes me tries hard to be cheerful, to not mention my illness, to tell me what is going on in Dresden. I don't remember much of the past year . . .

Dear Norma,

I'm glad to hear about your book. I'm looking forward to reading your poetry. I have been working on the after madness poems. I still can't read the during madness ones.. . .

Dear Norma,

Roanoke isn't near Williamsburg . . .

Dear Norma,

The "Cookie Cutter Life" is a powerful poem. What do you know about such stuff? . . .

Dear Stephen,

I got a letter from Norma Harrison. Why did your Department Chair's wife write me? . . .

Dear Norma,

It was so good to hear from you. It was especially good to hear that you have a new book of poems coming out. I don't know when I'm coming back to Dresden. . . .

Dear Anne Macklin,

You don't know me. My husband works with your husband in the English Department. . . .

Dear Joyce,

Norma suggested I write to you and let you know before anyone else did—Jack and I are separated. It's all for the best. Things have never been the same since his bloody fight for tenure and his fight to get his book finished. He was so busy doing that for himself that he never noticed what was happening to me and the children. I felt like a single parent. You're lucky not to have any children. On top of that, I had to handle everything about the house.

Enough of the gloom. The separation is working out well. As a matter of fact, the boys see more of their father now than before.

I am also writing you because I had a cup of coffee with Stephen the other day. He looked down in the dumps and said he was having trouble sleeping. Sounds like he's missing his wife.

Hope to see you soon.

Anne

Dear Anne,

How strange, I don't feel lucky. I'm sorry but Norma beat you to it. I know about the separation. . . .

Dear Stephen,

Mother is fine. She's a grand ole girl. Full of life and spice. We take short walks in the woods. The weather is so balmy. I have forgotten how different the weather down South is from the North. Can you believe that Mother put up preserves last fall? There are jars and jars of pickled peaches and spiked apples. She treats me like a little girl too. I sleep in the same gingham room I had when I was twelve. Someday maybe I will have a daughter. . . .

Dear Joyce,

Hope you are getting stronger and enjoying your time in sunnier climes. I miss our talks at Wendy's over a burger. I know they helped me. I hope they helped you.

How are you feeling about coming back to Dresden? I'm not asking as a psychologist but as your friend. The pressures aren't going to be any easier, in fact they will be harder because everyone in this tiny community knows you had a breakdown. I'd suggest you get yourself in with a therapist away from Dresden. I can recommend a woman at the Dartmouth Hitchcock Clinic in Hanover—Dr. Margot Feydeau.

Can't believe that Xanda will start kindergarten this fall. Guess Charlie and I are settling in here. Hope to see you soon.

Stay well. Darise

Dear Darise,

I'm so scared. I don't know if I want to come back. I know Stephen needs me but I'm still . . . .

Dear Darise,

Do you really think I can make a comeback? . . .

Dearest Joyce,

I miss you very much. The semester will be over in a few weeks. I want to drive down there. Maybe, Joyce, your doctor will say, it's okay for you to come back with me. By the time we get back, it will be spring in Dresden. I miss you.

Stephen

Dear Stephen,

I haven't been seeing a psychiatrist, just the regular M.D. . . .

Dear Stephen,

Mother stills tends her own flower garden. She dries flowers and makes rose water. She looks so very young for 76. I wonder if I will live to be . . . .

Darling Stephen,

Come swiftly my love and bring me home to you.

Joyce

IV Dresden in Several Scenes

Journal entry:

Summer was easy. Stephen wasn't teaching. It was the time when he went to the computer center and then to the library to work on his book in the mornings. Then we would go to the lake and he would swim and I would sunbathe. I made sandwiches and we had picnics. I listened to him tell tales of his exploits as a college student, only to discover later that he was telling me other people's tales. What I liked best was the fact that there were few social obligations. Bill and Norma Harrison were in England. I spent time with Darise and her daughter Xanda. I went once a week down to Dartmouth to talk to Margot Feydeau, my therapist. It was only when the fall semester began that the rigors of being a faculty wife kicked in.

Here's my attempt to show it in play form. I don't think that it is quite my style, any more than poetry is. Of course, if I was going to put the play on, I'd have to change everyone's name.

SETTING

Dresden, a small New England college town in the early eighties. Dresden is the home of an elite women's college.

CHARACTERS

Joyce	Wife of a tenure hopeful, early 30s
Stephen	Joyce's husband, mid-30s
Bill	English Department Chair, early 50s
Norma	Bill's wife, poet, mid-forties
Sheri	Wife of absent faculty member
Vincent	Black sociology professor
Ruth	Spouse of Vincent
Anne	Ex-spouse of tenured professor

SCENE 1 At home with Joyce and Stephen

JOYCE We need to talk.

STEPHEN Yes, we need to talk. Norma and Bill are having a small dinner party next week and we are invited. Cocktails before and then a sit-down dinner. Rick Riccibono wasn't invited. It's a good sign that we were. It may mean I get tenure.

JOYCE I know about the party. Norma called me.

STEPHEN Really. She called you?

JOYCE Yes. I told you she wrote me when I was in Virginia. I need to talk to you about my therapy. Dr. Feydeau would like you to come with me to at least one of my sessions.

STEPHEN I don't remember your saying that Norma wrote you. Did you write back to her? What did you say?

JOYCE Things are all right with Norma. I need you to listen to me, Stephen. We need to talk about my therapy. You want to help me, don't you?

STEPHEN Of course, I do. . . You do want me to get tenure, don't you?

JOYCE I want what you want, Stephen.

SCENE 2 In the car one week later

STEPHEN I'm sure you'll have a good time tonight. It's not a big party, just a few people from the college.

JOYCE I know this is important to you, Stephen, and that's why we are going to this party. How do you want me to behave with Norma? You once said that I shouldn't get too friendly with her.

STEPHEN I was wrong. Once all this tenure business is over, I'll go with you to the doctor down at Dartmouth Hitchcock Clinic.

JOYCE You promise.

STEPHEN I promise.

SCENE 3 Cocktails

NORMA Did you make your dress, Sheri?

SHERI Yes. Just a few alterations of a McCall pattern and this divine print we got when Jim and I were in Sierra Leone.

NORMA I never go anywhere. Bill vegetates here teaching Early American Literature while I write my little poems that no one reads.
SHERI Oh, I love your little poems.

JOYCE ENTERS

NORMA You didn't make your dress, did you, Joyce? Sheri made hers.
JOYCE No, Norma. I don't sew.
NORMA Where did you get it? Here in Dresden?
JOYCE No, in Roanoke at the Beyerkoff . . .

NORMA MOVES AWAY TO CIRCULATE

(To Sheri) The Beyerkoff is sort of the Saks Fifth Avenue of Virginia. (Joyce smiles to herself)
SHERI Like Neiman Marcus in Dallas? (whispering) Have you ever read any of her poems? They sound perverted to me. Didn't she have a breakdown? (Sheri blushes suddenly and her voice trails off) I guess I have her confused with someone else.
JOYCE No, you're perfectly right about one thing, she writes poetry.

SHERI CIRCULATES

SCENE 4 At dinner

VINCENT TO NORMA (Pointing to a painting on the wall in the dining room) Who's the attractive African woman in the painting?
NORMA Hate to disillusion you, but she isn't any more African than you are, Vincent, despite the clothing. Her name is Mira Mahou, and she was painted by a Black artist friend of mine. He supplied the clothes.
VINCENT It's clear she wears them well because of her natural heritage. I'm just surprised to see a painting like this on your walls.
NORMA There's a side of me that you know nothing about . . .

I come to you
after Mira Mahou

wearing her blue beret on
kinky hair dyed red
to share your bed worn brown
with colored bodies

THEY EAT IN RELATIVE SILENCE

VINCENT I believe that abortion is a form of genocide for Black people.

NORMA Then don't have one!

BILL Don't pay any attention to my wife, Vincent, she's a great joker.

NORMA What do you think, Ruthie? Do you agree with your husband?

RUTH Of course I agree with Vincent. I think that which has kept us strong as a—

VINCENT (Interrupting but continuing Ruth's sentence) —people is the family, the hope and promise of the Black family.

JOYCE But we don't have children and we support abortion for ourselves.

VINCENT You may not have children, but you have this. (He points to the silverware) You have this. (He points to the china plate half full of uneaten food) You have this. (He points to the necklace around Norma's neck)

RUTH And even though you may support abortion, you are not the ones getting sterilized and aborted.

STEPHEN You make it sound like it's being done to you instead of by you of your own choice. My wife and I have decided against children after two miscarriages and—

VINCEN (Interrupting) There it is, the same thing always happens. It's your problem. Your problems are not our problems. They're simply different.

JOYCE How can that be? Isn't an abortion just an abortion, no matter what woman has it?

NORMA Apparently not.

SCENE 5 After-dinner drinks

ANNE I'm applying to law school. There are still a few details to iron out in the divorce. Going to court was a real eye opener. I want to help other women.

NORMA Have you got a buyer for the house?

ANNE We aren't selling right now. (To Joyce) You know he's seeing Sally.

JOYCE Oh Anne!

ANNE It's all right. I guess you're the only one who didn't know. Right, Norma?

NORMA Joyce doesn't listen to gossip. (To Joyce) What have you been up to since you got back?

JOYCE I've been busy writing.

ANNE I'm going to leave the two of you to talk writing.

ANNE EXITS

NORMA Poetry?

JOYCE Just writing.

NORMA See, I told you that you'd be all right.

STEPHEN ENTERS

STEPHEN Ready to go home, Joycie? (To Norma) Thanks so much for your hospitality.

NORMA Call me, Joyce. I want to see how you're doing.

SCENE 5 In the car

STEPHEN I think it went very well. Every time I looked at you, you were talking to someone.

JOYCE How was it for you? Did Bill seem impressed with you?

STEPHEN I held my own. You like it here, don't you Joycie? You want to stay, don't you? You want me to get tenure, don't you?

JOYCE Of course I do, Stephen . . .

V A Booth at Wendy's

There's a Sondheim song, "The Ladies Who Lunch," and I imagine the fashionable women who live in New York City and eat at elegant restaurants or on a smaller scale the faculty wives of Dresden, the small New England college town where I live. These wives of the tenured faculty ensconce themselves at the buffet luncheon at the Dresden Inn.

Not like Darise and me. Wendy's is our place. It is within our price range unlike the Inn or the other high-priced restaurants of Dresden. Wendy's is about five miles west of Dresden near the shopping mall and the interstate in a world totally different from Dresden.

Darise and I have been having lunch at Wendy's at least once a month since we met in an exercise class conducted by a former ballerina who is the wife of the orchestral music professor at Amberton College. Darise caught my eye because she had her young daughter with her. Her daughter was so beautiful and charming that all the women in the class spent much of the time admiring her attempts to do the exercises with us. I don't remember who suggested we stop for coffee, most likely I did. It was unusual because most women had to run off and prepare dinner for their families. Darise said her husband, in addition to teaching, was also a recruiter for minorities and was out of town a great deal. My husband was in the computer center working on his book. We were both two lonely young women.

Darise was late. I didn't mind, I ordered a pot of coffee, took out my notebook, and started writing. I had something to talk to Darise about. She is a child psychologist, but I have been using her expertise to help me on my journey back to mental health.

I've come a long way since I came back from my mother's after suffering a nervous breakdown. At first I wasn't sure I was ready to come back to Dresden, but I felt I owed it to my husband who is up for tenure.

Darise arrived out of breath and looking harried.

"Where's Xanda?" I asked.

"Play group. Sorry I'm late," Darise said.

"It's okay."

Darise looked worried and tired.

"Are you okay?" I questioned.

"Difficult case," Darise explained.

"I know you can't talk about it So let me make this easier by changing the subject. I want to tell you something. I want you to listen and not say anything until I'm finished."

Darise smiled and said, "I'm not going to promise anything of the sort. You have to remember I'm a psychologist and I'm compelled to give advice."

"You'll have plenty of time to do just that. But as is my southern tradition, I have to tell my story . . . As you know, when Stephen and I came here to visit, we thought Dresden was paradise. I was pregnant and we thought this would be an ideal place where we could put down roots and a perfect place for our new family. I was surprised at how difficult it was for me to move from New York City to Dresden. I thought since I grew up in a small town in Virginia it would be easy to adjust to a small town again. But it wasn't. I missed New York. I missed my job as a librarian."

Even though I had told her this before, I continued. " When I moved to New York City against my mother's wishes, I was proud of myself. I believe I made a successful life for myself. I was an independent and self-sufficient person. It was a hard-won battle. Then I met Stephen, and he wanted to take care of me. I thought it was what I wanted, and it worked until we moved here and I didn't have a job anymore or anyone to talk to except Stephen. That was before we became friends.

I lost my identity as an individual and was nothing but Stephen's wife. And the unthinkable happened. I lost two babies. I was told that I mustn't blame myself. Things like this just happen and that we should try again to get pregnant. In the meantime, it was suggested that I see a psychiatrist. I was referred to Morgan Sumner. I think I asked Norma Harrison. She was one of the few friends I had made in Dresden even though she was married to Stephen's boss. Norma was like a big sister to me." Darise grimaced.

"I know that doesn't sound like Norma, but she really has been kind to me, and I think she is the reason that Stephen got an extension on his bid for tenure since her husband is head of the department. Norma is her own self, of course, like you. She's not just the department head's wife; she's a published poet. Lots of people, including you, don't know what she's really like. Don't get me started on Norma."

"I didn't get you off on Norma. I merely smiled," Darise said.

"It was more of a scowl. I need to talk about my therapy."

"Are you sure you want to do that, Joyce?"

"Darise, you're a therapist. Explain to me why Dr. Feydeau is so different from Morgan . . . I mean Dr. Sumner . . . All he wanted to talk about as far as I remember was my childhood, my parents, their marriage. Then too he gave me prescriptions for lots of drugs. Feydeau doesn't believe in drugs. She says taking pills won't get to the underlying problem. She's always asking me how I feel about the miscarriages, my relationship with Stephen. She keeps asking me how I feel about living in Dresden and what tenure for Stephen will mean for me."

"Have you thought about any of the things Dr. Feydeau asked you?"

"Yes. But I don't know how I feel. Morgan and Dr. Feydeau are so different. Which one is right?"

"Why does one of them have to be right? Think about what happened to you when you stopped seeing Morgan Sumner."

"I went mad."

"Do you feel that way now?" Darise sounded like a therapist.

I replied quickly, "No, not at all. I don't want to let Stephen down again . . . And I have my writing now."

"Joyce, I'm sorry but I have to pick up Xanda in ten minutes. Can we continue tomorrow?"

"No, I can't," I said.

"Wednesday?" she asked.

"Okay, Darise. You promise to be on time."

"I promise."

***

It took nearly three weeks for us to get back together. This time I was late. I was eager to tell Darise all that I had learned about myself, but she seemed preoccupied and sad.

"Why can't we both be in the same mood at the same time?" I asked.

"It doesn't work like that even with married people," Darise said.

"Tell me about it," I joked.

"You look like you are having a great day," Darise remarked.

"I was, until I saw your gloomy face."

"Tell me what has made you so happy," Darise said, her look changing slightly.

"I had a marvelous breakthrough in my writing."

"Your writing is going well?" Darise had a wistful smile on her face.

"My writing helps me uncover things about myself. Helps me know things and understand things. Mostly, I have been keeping a journal. I haven't quite found my genre yet. At first I thought it was poetry. . . . Darise, are you up to listening to me?"

"Yes." She paused a moment and took a sip of coffee. "Maybe I should begin to write too," she added.

"Darise, what's wrong? Tell me. You usually let me rattle on about myself. It's about time I listened to you."

"Joyce, I can't. If I started, I don't think I could stop. At least not today. Someday when we can talk uninterrupted for a long time, we can discuss relationships and marriage and what makes them work and not work. Maybe you'll find the answer to that mystery in your writing and be able to tell it to me."

"I don't know," I answer honestly. "Maybe, that's one for the therapist."

"In that case," Darise said, "psychologist heal yourself."

The waiter came, and I ordered a cheeseburger with fries and Darise as usual ordered a salad.

"I registered Xanda for kindergarten," she said as we waited for our food.

"It's hard to believe that she is ready for school," I answered.

"She was so excited, she thought she would start school tomorrow."

I started to tell Darise that I had liked school too. It wasn't surprising when both of your parents were teachers, like mine. I didn't say it though. A gloom had settled on us. I watched as she picked at her food. I had lost my appetite as well.

The waiter came and asked us if we wanted to take the food home in a doggy bag. We both declined.

"See you at exercise class," I called as we parted in the parking lot.

It was a bright sunny day but some of her sadness had rubbed off on me and lasted for the rest of the day. When I sat down at my desk to write, I could not escape the look of despair I had glimpsed on Darise's face, and then it came to me that it was the first time in ages that I had noticed and been affected by someone else's mood. It made me weep. I wasn't sure if it was for myself or her.

VI Arranging Flowers

Journal entry:

It's Dresden weather—that means there may be a snowstorm tomorrow or people will be walking around in shirtsleeves. I'm encouraged by the fact that a few hardy flowers and green shoots are visible when I take my daily walk.

I'm on the road to recovery. I'm sure of it. It's not just seeing Dr. Feyedeau at Dartmouth Hitchcock Clinic instead of Morgan Sumner at the Rebecca Amberton Mental Health Center. Perhaps it wasn't the wisest idea to see a therapist here in Dresden while my husband was seeking tenure, but that's water under the bridge. And today something wonderful happened. The well-known author and alumna Philomena Dodsworth Taylor is going to teach a ten-day pre-summer term course in the Art of the Short Story and I want to audit it.

I am going to write today. To write something I can submit to P. D. Taylor in order to enroll in the class. Of course I can't use any of my earlier writing. I have kept the notebooks and poetry I wrote, but it all seems a part of my madness. Instead I'm going to write a short story.

Mother Arranging Flowers
by
Joyce Pantara
"Judith Marie," her mother called. It seemed to her that her mother was always calling, always beckoning her back from some imaginary adventure, some place in a book or in a daydream.

"Yes, Mother," she answered. She had suddenly realized that only southerners said "Yes, Ma'am." She didn't want to ever sound like a southerner, even though she was one. No, not in a world where Ann Elizabeth Beech, her classmate, had already been to Paris, France.

It was also southern to say the full names of things like Paris, France, or Ann Elizabeth Beech. She (Judith Marie Applewaite) wanted to be cosmopolitan and sophisticated like people who lived in New York City. She didn't want to be like every teen in America with her hair in a ponytail and wearing jeans and a letter jacket. Nor did she want to be like Lesley Gore, Ricky Nelson, or the Mouseketeers. She didn't blend into the teen movies or melt into the rock music on the radio. Instead, she wanted to sip wine in a dark Greenwich Village jazz club and read her poetry aloud to its denizens.

"Judith Marie, don't you hear me calling you?" came the shrill voice of her mother.

Journal Entry:

Should I describe Judith? Maybe I'd better wait until she and her mother meet. I haven't as yet worked out what I am going to do with the two of them, but I'll think of something.

***

Judith bounded down the stairs two at a time. At fourteen she was caught up in the conflict of wanting to go down the stairs with the old freedom of her tomboy self, but knew that it was no longer seemly to do so.

Mrs. Applewaite, her mother, was a small birdlike woman with nervous hands and dyed red hair. She was over fifty, and perhaps the only thing that saved her from looking old was that she was, as she liked to say, très petite. Her mother, Samara Louise, had been the high school French teacher for years before she "up and married" newly widowed Aloysius Applewaite. No one in town had liked his first wife. People thought her arrogant and foreign looking. She rarely left the Applewaite house on Beacham Road and never accepted guests. Samara Louise was a hometown girl that everyone knew. The marriage between the two teachers—Aloysius and Samara Louise was greeted with moderate approval.

Journal Entry:

I'm getting away from the main point. This is a story about a mother and daughter. It is also a thinly disguised story of my parents and me. I've changed the names basically. Should I change anything else? No one, not even Stephen knows all of this.

***

The townspeople liked Aloysius and believed that he should remarry. Samara Louise didn't seem the appropriate choice. People whispered that she must be nearly forty if she was a day. She was fading in the way that many women do who have dreams of being coquettes but lead lives as shopkeepers and schoolteachers. Women whose lives were worn heavily on their heads instead of frilly hats and tortoiseshell combs.

Samara Louise had hoped to travel, but travel for her was limited to a two-week tour of England and France with a YWCA group—churches and museums and a clergyman and his wife as guides. Samara still lived with her mother and father on a side street away from the most fashionable part of town where Aloysius's family home was. She lived among her postcards and reproductions of the two glorious weeks she had spent abroad.

On the other hand, Aloysius had spent most of his life in a comfortable and roomy home with its study lined with books, The only exception was a short period when he studied in Belgium. He had missed military service because of a heart murmur and gone overseas to study the classics at the University of Antwerp. Once he returned, he never seemed to wish to travel anywhere else. He had met the dark-eyed, dark haired Judith Levy at a teachers convention in Richmond and married her after several months of long-distance courting. And just as suddenly, Judith died and Aloysius was left alone in the big house on Beacham.

The marriage between Samara Louise and Aloysius, the two high school teachers, was somewhat of a shock, but before the townspeople could adjust to it came the earth-shattering news of the pregnancy.

At the first news of her pregnancy, Samara Louise quit

teaching. Then a miracle occurred; Samara grew young. She became strong—she worked in the garden that surrounded the house. She knitted and sewed clothes for the baby (all blue; she was convinced it would be a boy). She opened the house that had been noted for its closed shutters and mystery. She attended the First Presbyterian Church alongside her husband. By the time the baby arrived, people were openly saying that Samara was actually in her thirties and not a decade older.

The baby girl was red-faced and suffered from colic. She was a cranky baby, all of which her mother accepted with blissful quietude. For some reason known only to the two of them, the girl was given the same name as Aloysius's first wife.

Judith Marie had few memories of her father. She remembered tiptoeing around the house so as not to disturb him. He seemed to spend most of the time in his study with the door closed. Once she had burst into the room without knocking to find him at his desk with an open notebook in front of him. Tears streamed down his face. She thought it strange that no sound came from his lips because when she cried she always made lots of noise.

Then one winter night a strange ice storm hit the valley; Aloysius's car broke down on a country road miles away from town. No one knew why he was there. Apparently, he died of exposure. Samara Louise showed what she was made of with this tragedy. She returned to teaching and hired a colored girl to live in and care for the house and Judith. Samara even began to dye her hair, but everyone accepted it because in those days she had to appear younger in order to keep her teaching job.

Judith Marie looked at her mother who stood in the kitchen at the sink. She had collected several vases from around the house and place them on the kitchen table. She washed them, filled them with cool vinegar water, and in them placed fresh flowers she had cut from her garden.

Taking a risk, Judith Marie asked her mother, "How did you get Daddy to notice you?"

"He didn't at first. I just waited until he was ready. Men operate on their own timetable. When it's time, a man will seek you out, no matter where you are and choose you, if it is meant to be."

Judith Marie wanted to protest. Bryson would never choose her. She wasn't pretty or bouncy like the cheerleaders. It was a mistake to ask her mother. Her mother was too old, too interested in her flowers to know or care about love.

"Tell me about Daddy," Judith Marie said.

"He was a very scholarly man. A very sensitive man. Too sensitive for the hard cruel world we live in."

"What does that mean?" the teenager asked.

"You are a lot like him, I'm afraid. I wish you were tougher. If not, I hope you find someone to protect you. It's like the rose—see how beautiful it is. It is a delicate flower but it has to have thorns to surround and protect it from the harshness of the world."

"Do you think I'm a rose?" Judith Marie questioned. "Where are my thorns?"

"I'm your thorns for now. I always have been and will be until the right man comes along who will protect and keep you all of your life."

Journal Entry:

When I was banished to my mother's after my breakdown, I would look at the elderly woman she had become. I remembered that conversation we had had when I was a teenager about her being my protector like the thorns were to a rose. It was hard to think of her as a protector even though my husband had sent me to her as an antidote to my madness. There in her house that smelled of dried flowers, I had the chance to recuperate and be her child again for a while. Still, there is something wrong with this picture I'm painting.

***

"Mother, do you know Bryson Partridge? He's a senior. (Sometimes it helped to have a mother who is a teacher at the high school.)

"He is taking French Four, I believe. Good student. Isn't he

Marcus and Abigail's son?"

"I don't know, Mother." Judith began to wonder if it was a bad idea to talk to her mother about boys.

"Mother, I don't care who he's related to. He's very handsome. He plays the cello. I mean, he's a sensitive kind of boy, not like the rest of his classmates."

"And you like him?"

"Sort of. He doesn't know me from a doorknob."

"Don't give your heart to a sensitive boy. It will bring nothing but grief," her mother warned.

"But you said Daddy was sensitive."

"That's different. Even though I loved him long before we married, we did marry. I did have you. It was worth it."

Suddenly, Judith Marie lashed out. "I don't know why I bother to talk to you. What do you know? All you do is arrange your boring flowers. It drives me crazy. I bet it drove Daddy crazy too."

Her mother dropped the vase and the water and flowers spilled onto the floor. Pain and hurt reflected in her blue eyes. Judith Marie stepped away from her mother as if to dodge a blow that never came. They never spoke of boys again, nor of her father.

Journal Entry:

How ironic under the circumstances that she should speak of craziness — her father's craziness when she would one day be mad herself. Was my father mad? Is that where my insanity found its roots? The story of his death, seems to be just that — a story. Why was he so unhappy, so desperately unhappy that he killed himself. If in fact, he did. What caused this unhappiness? My mother? Were they sexually incompatible? Was he a homosexual? My mother said he was sensitive. Was that a code word for being a homosexual?

I'm not sure I need to answer these questions in order to write this story. I think the answers are more about my life than about writing. I choose to write! I wish I could hole up for days and just write and write. No life but just writing. It would be fantastic. Not just this story, but the act of writing is my way back to sanity.

VII Playing Games

It was game night. I cleared the table quickly even though the leftover food was still warm in the pots. I wondered how many meals I had made, how many times I had cleared the table, washed the dishes. It was the rhythm of everyday life, but there was more to our lives than that. Stephen was off in the living room, setting up the table with the Scrabble board. That night it was Scrabble, the next week maybe Trivial Pursuit, and the next Monopoly. The games were part of our lives.

Game night meant board games, not card games. Mostly it was Rick Riccibono who is in the foreign language department — Italian, Spanish, and Latin and his girlfriend of the moment. One night my friend Darise, a child psychologist, and her husband Charles, another Amberton assistant professor, took Rick and his girlfriend's place on game night. We played Trivial Pursuit that night. Darise commented as they were leaving, "Stephen has a real killer instinct. I didn't know anyone could be more competitive than Charles."

"Stephen," I called, "Help me with the dishes."

"I'm setting up things. Rick will be here soon."

It wasn't that I wanted Stephen to actually help me with the dishes. I wanted him to be with me before the combat began. Lately, game night had become an imposition to me. I wanted to be writing instead. I hated anything that took me away from my writing. I felt surer of myself when I was writing. More than when I was fulfilling my function as the wife of an assistant professor, the woman of the house, and the otherwise responsible person. It was as though I was split in half — a me who cooked and cleaned and a me who wrote. Because of my past history, it frightened me to think of myself in that fragmented way.

"Stephen, don't you have papers to correct?" I asked.

"Worked on some this afternoon. Will burn the midnight oil .

. ." Suddenly he appeared before me in the doorway that connected the kitchen to the living room.

" Joyce, about Rick," Stephen began. "He didn't get the extension he asked for and will not be considered for tenure. He's looking for a new position. Worst case, he doesn't get something at MLA this summer. Best chance for a job is when you still have one."

"Does he know about your getting tenure?"

"I haven't talked about it, but he probably has heard through the grapevine."

"Shouldn't you tell him yourself? He's your friend. Don't you talk?"

"No. Guys don't behave like that."

I wanted to argue with him, that he wasn't like other guys. I stopped myself. Stephen liked to think of himself as one of the regular guys.

He sat down on the stool at the counter in the center of the kitchen.

"Joyce, you don't get it. I don't think you've ever wanted anything as much as I wanted tenure. I couldn't think of anyone or anything else, just that."

I started to tell him that I once had desired a baby that much, but didn't anymore. Now I wanted to finish my book and to know I could write forever.

Instead I said, "Who is Rick bringing tonight?"

"Tricia. I think she's in the dean's office."

"Really. I think he's trying to make it through the entire secretarial staff."

"At least he keeps his hands off the undergraduates," Stephen quipped.

I looked at Stephen's face. Sometime, when I wasn't aware, the boyish innocence had faded. His gray eyes were clouded and troubled. I thought of these years we had been together and all the losses we suffered. Perhaps the thing I didn't want to remember but did was his face at the hospital when I tried to kill myself. There were gray streaks in his sideburns. This winter he'll be thirty-six years old. I never saw my father when he was thirty-six nor my mother.

"What were you thinking about just now?" he asked me.

"Oh, nothing," I said.

"You were staring at me so intently."

"I was just thinking that time goes by, and we don't remember where it went. I'm going to be thirty-three in three weeks. Can you believe it?"

"Yes," he laughed. "What do you want for your birthday?"

"I don't know." I hesitated. "A chance of my own."

"What does that mean?"

"A chance for my own success," I answered.

It was clear that what I said somehow troubled him. I felt I should go to him and comfort him and ask his forgiveness for all that I had done to him.

"This is a time for us to be happy," he said suddenly. "I did it. We did it."

Just as he kissed me, the doorbell rang. Rick and Tricia from the dean's office arrived.

Tricia was a young woman, just barely in her twenties. She had very short dark hair and pale blue eyes that were accented with dark eyeliner and blue eye shadow. Rick proffered two six packs of beer, and Stephen popped out two cans and offered one to Rick.

"Beer or wine?" I asked Tricia.

"A beer," Tricia said.

I was the only one drinking wine. A large tray of onion dip and chips, pretzels, and slices of carrots, celery, and broccoli was on a side table. Only the Scrabble board was on the card table in the middle of the room.

Stephen started the game. He put down the letters Z-E-P-H-Y-R for a score of fifty-four.

"Wow," Tricia said. This was her first night at our house playing games, so she didn't know that we didn't comment or congratulate.

Stephen had used six of his seven letters to start off with. It was the largest beginning score I had ever seen. Tonight was going to be rough. I wanted to quit.

"Can I put down B-I on top of the Z to make BIZ?" asked Tricia who was next.

"Biz is not an acceptable Scrabble word," Rick said beating Stephen to the punch of that recitation of rules.

Building up off the P, Tricia put down L-I-P for a score of seven.

It was my turn. I added two Os down from the Z for a score of twelve.

"Well, that fouls it up for a real word," Rick said testily.

He was last. Rick added an S to ZEPHYR and the word HUGS earned him thirty-one points.

It was back to Stephen. "No chance of a triple word score off ZEPHYR," he quipped, "thanks to Rick."

From the H, he spelt HEIST for a score of sixteen.

Tricia shrugged her shoulders. It was clearly not what she considered a fun evening. She used the letter N to make NO off the last O in ZOO.

I put a K in front of Tricia's NO and a T after it to make KNOT for eighteen points.

Rick's eyes were gleaming as he placed a Q on a double letter space for a score of twenty points. He made the word QUOTE for a double word score of forty-eight. He was ahead of Stephen. It was clearly a contest between the two of them. Tricia and I were accessories and at times minor irritants when we took the place that either of them had plans for creating high-scoring words.

Rick and Stephen reminded me of a cartoon movie I saw as a child. Two gigantic bucks with enormous racks of antlers clashed in darken silhouettes. It had frightened me then and it frightened me now. In the end Stephen was defeated by Rick. In the process we consumed great quantities of chips, dip, beer, and wine.

"Guess this is the last get-together of the year," Rick said. He waited a moment and added, "And if I'm lucky, I won't be back. I have an interview at Boulder State."

"You mean you're going to leave believing you are the all-time champ," Stephen said.

"I beat you this time by nineteen points," Rick said in a subdued manner.

Tricia stood next to me at the door impatient to leave and begin the night. I had the feeling she would like to see Boulder too, though I doubted she would.

"Thank you for your hospitality," she said in my direction.

After they left, Stephen asked, "Are you coming to bed?"

"No."

"Why not?"

" I want to write. I need to finish something."

"No, Joyce. Let this be our celebration for my getting tenure. Let's make a baby."

"Stephen, oh no. Two miscarriages in two years. I thought we decided not to have any children."

"It's different now," he insisted, "I got tenure and you're back to normal like those breakdowns never happened," Stephen said.

"But they did happen, Stephen. They happened and they made me who I am now."

"Who are you? Aren't you still Joyce, my wife? Aren't you still the woman, I married?"

"I don't know, Stephen. I know that I can't live like this anymore. I have to do some meaningful work —— not just hang around here like a perpetual invalid."

"Most women would love to stay home," Stephen began and then stopped himself.

"Joycie, don't you want to have a baby?" he crooned in his most seductive voice.

"We're talking in circles, Stephen."

"So it was okay for us to have a baby when you were making a fool of me and yourself, but not now when we have a future. You owe me! I stuck by you. Rick told me I should leave your fucking crazy ass. But I was loyal and true to you."

"If that's how you feel, why do you want to have a baby with me?"

"I deserve to have a good life, a home, a child to go along with my career," Stephen said. Mixed in with the anguish of his plea was the sound of menace. For a moment I stood silently watching my husband in all his complexity as though for the first time. I thought about earlier in the evening before we had begun to play games when I had ruminated about my life with Stephen. There was a routine of the accepted and the expected that was what life was supposed to be. It was safe and predictable. Without speaking anymore I followed Stephen to bed with a confused and guilty heart.

VIII Joyceday

Journal entry:

I turned over in bed and reached for my journal. it was just a little past dawn. I was used to sleeping alone. However, Stephen was not down the hall in the master bedroom. He was out of town at a weekend seminar. This was not the first time we have slept in separate bedrooms in our marriage. The other times were different. I had spiraled out of control and slept away from Stephen to keep myself safe from him or keep him safe from me. I was never sure which was true.

Then, all time melted into one. Midnight, three A.M., dawn, ten-thirty A.M. I couldn't keep track of the days of the week either. I saw my psychiatrist Morgan Sumner three times a week. And these sessions weren't enough.

Once I ran away to Boston and picked up a stranger in a bar in Harvard Square. I brought him to my hotel room and had sex with him. I felt nothing but disgust for myself and tried to kill myself.

"Who's Morgan?" the stranger asked me.

"Why?"

"You keep calling me that name."

For a long time I had little memory of what happened in that hotel room. It's still painful to think of it. I reached for my purse after the stranger left. I had brought every pill bottle that I had in my house with me. I took all of the pills. The last thing I remember was dialing a number. It must have been Morgan's. He turned up in my room. It smelled of vomit. Morgan saved me. I survived. Morgan sent me home to my husband. I never told Stephen about the stranger or that Morgan had saved me that time. I think it would have changed things between us if I had. Stephen waited for me to get better and then when I tried to kill myself again, he sent me south to my mother. It took me a long time before I was lucid enough to be angry with Stephen for sending me to my mother.

It's time to get up and stop writing.

Journal Entry:

I went into Sean Daedalus's room. He stood in his crib. Believe it or not, he's a happy baby. Time goes by swiftly with him. He is resting now, so I can write in here again. I wonder how he can be so well adjusted — after all, he is the product of his half-mad mother and his angry, hurt father. But there is still love between Stephen and me. Sean Daedalus is like some magic wonderul gift that we share.

Now that Stephen, the baby, and I live outside of Dresden, my life is quite different. I don't walk much. I have learned how to drive and have a beat-up old Chevy Vega. I have become a gardener, a decorator, a cook, and homemaker. I do all those things with a yeoman's diligence, but little zeal. Two days a week, I drive into Dresden to the "Mommy and Me Swim classes." Sean Daedalus is a happy baby. Sean makes me laugh and forget how things between Stephen and me really are.

Once, Norma Harrison, a poet and wife of the head of the department, wrote me a letter and told about another couple's divorce.

She said, "I've never seen it to fail. He gets tenure, they buy the house, the children are doing well in school, and then things fall apart."

What fell apart for Stephen and me? On the surface we seemed to have found the key to a stable happy life, after years of struggle. Still things fell apart.

Was it the day I told him the truth about what happened in Boston? He was angry certainly, but I don't think a man or woman came between us. I think it was my writing that did that. Not the writing that I did when I first came to Dresden. I filled notebooks with the ramblings of my madness. I walked around Dresden with my notebook clasped close to me. For weeks I walked to the post office from our faculty apartment to get the mail and to mail off my poetry to obscure literary magazines. I went to the Dresden Stop'n Shop to buy the New York papers. There were menacing voices in my head and I was beset by demons that made me feel unsafe and unloved. I had a steak knife in my jacket pocket to protect myself.

I was afraid then and I'm afraid now but of different things. I was afraid then because I felt myself being swallowed up by Dresden and Amberton College. I seemed to be disappearing. I had no work, no purpose, and I had had two miscarriages. Stephen's battle for tenure seemed like his own personal struggle.

Writing was the turning point in my life. Stephen got tenure and we bought a house and had a baby. The baby's name, Sean Daedalus, was chosen by Stephen for its literary allusions. He even joked that the baby was partially a Joyce creation. Stephen was pleased with himself. He had weathered the storm of his crazy wife and now was reaping the rewards.

These events and my writing were on two parallel courses with very little to do with each other. I had discovered that poetry might have suited my insanity but fiction was what I loved. After auditing a short story writing course with P. D. Taylor, the prize-winning writer and alumna of Amberton College, I began to write stories and send them to small magazines. When one of my stories was published in The New England Literary Journal, Stephen was informed by a colleague.

"Joyce, why didn't you tell me that your story was coming out in the NELJ? Brenda, you know her, she's Feminism and Bloomsbury, accosted me in the Common Room. For a moment, I thought she was asking me about my essay on Emerson."

"I thought I told you about my story," I replied.

"Any others I need to be on the lookout for?"

"Not right now," I answered. Three others had appeared in literary magazines farther away from home.

"Taking care of Daedalus and the new house probably doesn't leave you much time for anything else," Stephen said.

"Not exactly," I began. "I am putting together my stories to make a collection."

"How many do you have?" He looked up with something like alarm on his face.

"Quite a few," I confessed.

"That'll take some time, I imagine. I know how difficult it is to put something like that together. Take my essays on the transcendental poets," Stephen said.

He went back to his papers, and I never told him that I had put the stories together already and sent them off to a small press in Minnesota.

Six months ago my short story collection was accepted for publication. Stephen was away on an intense weekend seminar. I bought a small bottle of champagne and toasted my good fortune. At first I felt guilty about sitting there alone and enjoying the moment of triumph on my own. I should have been sharing it with my husband. But I knew Stephen somehow or other would twist it around so that it would be about him and his accomplishments. This was mine, all mine, and I celebrated it for me.

Norma Harrison had a little reception for me. Stephen was gracious and complimentary as he greeted his colleagues at the reception. We never discussed the fact that I had written mostly in secret and that he had never read any of the stories except perhaps, the story that Brenda, "Feminism and Bloomsbury," told him about.

"Do you think you're a writer?" Stephen questioned me after the reception.

"Norma writes," I said defensively.

"The truth about Norma is that she takes it to the edge, but she only does that because Bill is department chair and has been tenured forever. Bill's position and money make it possible for her to live her life the way she does . . . Joyce, you must see that this can embarrass me . . . A few stories in some obscure journals is okay and maybe years from now, teaching an extension course at a junior college when Daedalus is older . . . You have a history after all."

I wanted to ask him would my success be an embarrassment?

Stephen thought that this talk had put a finish to my writing. So, he didn't worry about it for a while. We talked about painting the deck, gardening, and toilet training Sean.

Once Stephen and I went down to New York for a convention and to show off Sean to Stephen's family. His parents were dead, but an elderly aunt and an ancient grandmother who spoke only Italian met Sean Daedalus Pantara and me. Through Norma, I got a meeting with a literary agent. Her name was Eileen Mansfield of the Mansfield and Brock Literary Agency.

"Have you ever thought of writing a novel?" Eileen, the tall smartly dressed redhead asked me.

"Not really. I feel like I'm still mastering the short story."

"That's all well and good in an artistic sense, but the market for stories is dwindling and almost dry. Besides, I can see the 'seeds' of a novel in your short stories collection," she continued.

"Are you saying you're interested in representing me only if I write a novel?"

"I find you a promising writer. I think you need to take the next step," she told me.

Journal Entry:

I want to clarify things and writing this helps me. After that I came back to Dresden shaken, because I knew deep inside of me I wanted success as a writer as much as I wanted anything. Having Sean Daedalus was a fulfillment of a dream, but success as a writer was a secret desire that overpowered me. Success seemed to be in New York. Norma concurred.

"Go," she said at lunch at the Dresden Inn.

"Why didn't you go?"

"I was too old and too chicken. Besides, I don't have your talent."

"I always thought of you as brave," I said in a shocked voice.

"Well, I'm not. All I do is have meaningless affairs and write poems about them."

"Does Bill . . . ?"

"Does Bill know?" Norma interrupted. "He knows and he doesn't. Don't feel sorry for him. He has had his share. But we always wind up with each other. That's all we have. Take care of your son. Do this for him!"

"I have to do this for myself, first of all." I had made a decision at that moment. I reached out and touched Norma's hand. Her eyes were full of tears.

I have to stop here.

Journal Entry:
Just when I thought the most important thing to deal with was moving back to New York and separating from my husband, another element was introduced into the mix. In the Dresden Spectator was the obituary for my former psychiatrist — Morgan Sumner.

Dr. Morgan Marcus Sumner died in his home in Dresden on May 4, 1985. Dr. Sumner was born in Hastings on the Hudson, New York, on August 2, 1932, to Dr. Thornton Marcus and Agatha (Newton) Sumner.

After graduation from Phillips Exeter Academy, he attended Cornell University and Cornell Medical School. He received a Ph.D. from the Psychoanalytical Institute of Boston.

Dr. Sumner is survived by his mother Agatha of Melbourne, Florida, his sister Dr. Sarah Sumner-Bingham of Scarsdale, New York, and his former wife, Pamela Ashford-Grimes of Dresden, and his nieces and nephews.

He was predeceased by his father, Dr. Thornton Marcus, and brother, Matthew William Sumner. Funeral services

will be private. A memorial service will be held for Dr.
Sumner at the Amberton College Chapel on May 24th
at 4 p.m. Contributions can be sent in Dr. Sumner's
name to the National Alliance for Mental Health.

I called my friend Darise immediately. Darise knew Morgan
and that he had been my doctor during my early days in Dresden.
Darise was with a patient but returned my call a half hour later.

"What do you know about Morgan, I mean Dr. Sumner's
death?" I asked.

"It's all right to call him Morgan. You always did . . . He
committed suicide, Joyce."

"No . . . Was he terminally ill or something?"

"I don't think he was physically ill . . . I didn't know him well
enough to know what his psychic pains were."

"He always seemed so self-possessed," I told her. "So sure of
himself . . . He talked me down once," I explained to Darise.

I knew she understood that I meant Morgan had talked me
through a suicide attempt.

"I went to Boston. I hooked up with some guy in a cafe
in Harvard Square and wound up taking a lot of pills . . . I will
never understand why I went to Boston. Boston is not my town.
You know, I love New York. Maybe I went because subconsciously
I remembered that Morgan was going to be there that weekend. I
called him before I passed out. He got to me before I did any serious
damage to myself."

"That's a very bonding experience," Darise said to me. "Joyce,
that was years ago. You couldn't have saved him."

"I know," I replied, the doubt clearly in my voice.

"It's all right to feel sad and mourn his loss. He was a significant
part of your life. Do you want to go to the memorial service? I can
go with you."

"I'll probably be in New York before the service takes place,

I replied.

"Oh, I see," Darise said. "When will you be leaving?"

"In a few days."

"Is Stephen back home yet?"

"No. We decided it would be better if he came back after Sean and I were gone."

"Did the two of you decide that or did you?"

"I guess I did," I revealed to Darise.

"Are you sure this is what you want?" she questioned.

"You are such a good therapist, Darise, I'm sure you know the answer to that question. I'm not certain what I want. When you and Charles split up and you stayed here and he left, were you sure you were doing the right thing?"

"Of course, I considered leaving, but it was different for me. I had my work and an identity independent of his. Still, it was/is difficult. This isn't a place for a single woman, especially a black one," Darise said.

"You've done very well here in Dresden," I told her. "But I need to build a life that doesn't impinge on Stephen's. I owe him that. Dresden is his home, his place," I explained.

"That sounds very noble," Darise countered.

"Darise, I'm just doing the best I can. I'm scared shitless. I'm not sure of anything. Eileen, my agent, got me an advance on a novel. I have a sublet while this Columbia professor is on sabbatical. It may be a big mistake and I may try to run back to Dresden with my tail between my legs. Nothing is sure except I have to take this chance to find the real me."

"Joyce, I think if it is possible, it might be good for you to attend Morgan Sumner's memorial service."

"But, Darise, Stephen will be back then. I don't think I can handle everything at the same time."

"You can have an opportunity to reach a certain amount of closure in two important aspects of your life. Of course, Stephen will always be in your life because of Sean," Darise reminded me.

Journal entry:

Being there made me think of the first time I had been in the chapel at Amberton. It was the memorial services for the then-president's daughter. Stephen and I sat together and held hands. It was all so new, so raw — we had just lost our first child. Oh, Stephen dealt with it by calling it a miscarriage or the lost of a fetus. We never talked about it, so I shouldn't have blamed him for not caring as much as I did.

When Stephen returned to Dresden and heard about Morgan's death, he said, "I really didn't know Dr. Sumner. I don't think it would be appropriate for me to attend his memorial service."

The last few days Stephen and I were exceedingly polite with each other and made certain that we gave each other space. The most interaction we had was playing with Sean Daedalus. It was the way most of our marriage had progressed, especially when I was sane. We always walked on eggshells. Soon even this forced politeness would be over.

The memorial service was brief. Dr. Kathleen Drinkwater, head of the Amberton Mental Health Clinic and Morgan's ex-wife, spoke. No one mentioned the fact that he was a suicide. He was presented as a complicated man who cared about people and quietly contributed to numerous mental health charities. He also had begun to counsel individuals and their families dealing with the scourge of AIDS.

Darise was right about attending the memorial service. I was able to bid Morgan goodbye and make a promise to myself and to Sean Daedalus that he would never have to sit in a chapel mourning his mother who had killed herself.

I quietly left the chapel. I couldn't bring myself to say goodbye to Darise. I promised myself to call her or write from New York. I promised that I would do the same for Norma. Both of these women had been true friends. I would see them again. I was just going to New York. We would not lose touch. I had not closed all the doors—not like Morgan had.

I left the chapel and walked into the sunlight of a new day.

About the Author

Deloris H. Netzband has an advanced degree in English and American Literature from New York University and has taught Literature and Creative Writing in college and secondary schools. She also has an advanced degree in Counseling and worked as a school counselor in several New Hampshire elementary schools. Deloris is one of the founders and the Associate Editor of Bloodroot Literary Magazine. Her stories have been shaped by three places: New York City, Cairo, Egypt and Hanover, New Hampshire. Stories of these places and people have appeared in literary magazines and journals for decades.

NET Netzband Delori
Netzband, Deloris H.
Dresden suite

DATE DUE			
5/5/17			
7/8/19			
2/24/21			

CPSIA information can be obtained
at www.ICGtesting.com
Printed in the USA
FFOW04n1848150514
5414FF

2015